We Live for Half-Moons

Weasel

A THURSTON HOWL PUBLICATIONS BOOK

ISBN 978-1-945247-03-3

WE LIVE FOR HALF-MOONS

We Live for Half-Moons © 2016 by Weasel

Edited by Rachel Raimondi
Book design by Arbor W. Barrow.

First Edition, 2016. All rights reserved.

A Thurston Howl Publications Book
Published by Thurston Howl Publications
thurstonhowlpublications.com
Jackson, TN

Mailing address:
51 Friars Point Rd, Apt H,
Jackson, TN, 38305
jonathan.thurstonhowlpub@gmail.com

Printed in the United States of America
10 9 8 7 6 5 4 3 2 1

"You know, you never fuck me, Derrick." Ely's words sputter about the room as we lie there in the nude, covers draped heavily over the sides. Ruffled cotton smoothed over by our subtle movement, growing like entangled weeds. I look at him, little lab mouse, twink body, totally fuckable. I don't have a reason for using him like the rest of his people do. Being a hooker can't be easy, even more so pretending to be somebody's friend in the middle of the night without the sex. At least with being a hooker, you can shrug it off, collect your cash, and go about your merry goddamn way. You want to keep your clients, but you don't want to get too attached.

He brings it up because he's afraid, I'm sure. His purpose is to provide a service. I am merely a client and should remain so. That's what clients do. We're not supposed to show regard for the person providing the service. They are merely the object or the means to get the object that we want.

I wonder how long I can keep him near before I start to get attached to him. I want him, but we are not meant to truly be with one another. He won't allow me to venture further inside him. I don't know why. He just wants the distance. He wants us both to be independent, but I'm not that kind of individual. I can't cling to independence yet, I'm not ready to see the new world that way. But it don't matter, changes happen. It's simply the way it goes.

I wonder what he sees when he looks at me. What do spots mean to the eyes of someone so fuckin' white. Does he know what monsters hide underneath dark brown spots and white fur? Does he know how tainted a person like me can become? My eyes tremble over his fur. Pure. I think of having sex with him, but I can't bring myself to do so. I let out a large sigh from my chest and turn to him.

"Yeah. I don't want to ruin you. There's too much beauty inside, and I can't be blamed for fuckin' up a good thing." It makes him uneasy, but there's a piece inside him that likes being complimented.

"My other clients…"

"Are people. They want what they want. Just like I do, and this is what I want. I told ya from the beginning."

The silence grows distant between us. Little Lab Mouse makes his peace with it and stares up at the ceiling.

This is how it always is between us. I get weak and call him over because I can't handle the noise in my home. There are too many fragments lingering around for me to truly escape, so I call this dude and open myself to him. There's no secrets, no sporadic confessions to give to the confessor. There's only time spent. That's what I pay him for, his time.

It's frightening to know that a single person can keep the darkest ghosts in your past, but Ely does. I'm not strong enough yet, and my neglect just makes it burn that much faster when I'm alone.

Little Lab Mouse is asleep now, the soft touch of his chest against my body inviting me to follow him. The stars are out tonight, one of the few times you can see them. The city is all too bright. My eyes slowly drift like clouds. The stars are gone as I meet him in our slumber.

Though I walk the valleys of my dreams, I still cannot escape the visions that have haunted me. The sun drapes over my fur, telling me it is morning. I know I am dreaming. I have had this one before. My body always shifts over to greet the other that shares my bed. He lays there, face drizzled with halos; it is how all the innocent sleep and he was no more evil than the old woman baking cookies for her grandkids up the street. Sweetest bitch I ever knew. This is how it always starts, and yet I am always surprised at the outcome. Such is the tragedy we hold inside ourselves.

We meander around, stubbing toes on cabinets, and cursing at flying bacon grease because our tempers are at war with our kitchen. He was simply a fox, orange tainting his fur, meshing with a white underbelly. We were groggy individuals, Nick even more so when it came to the early hours of the morning. Morning itself was early enough. His hair tousled like all hell, the black mess hung tangled as he worked over the stove. He said I could never cook right. He said I could only make sandwiches because they didn't need heat. Until the day I burned a grilled cheese sandwich. I got a fuckin' earful for that one, but that's life, ain't it? That was Nick— green pooling in his eyes, they were not something to be toyed with. He was never a toy.

I would sometimes drape my white fur with stigmata-like brown spots over him, and I could always hear him breathe my name in his personal silence. Even silence has a noise to it and his was whispered between crackles of grease and bacon.

"Derrick." The letters would linger as he turned off the stove and laid the plate on the table, his breakfast of which I stole pieces from each morning. And that is exactly how this dream starts. Though I know this is a dream, I still want to feel him. I still want to hear those whispers.

I'm at work now. It's a pharmacy school for the brightest kids that couldn't make it into prestigious universities, so they saddle themselves with hundreds of thousands of dollars in debt believing it'll pay off. I had some do-nothing office job making copies because I just had to be a fuckin' secretary. What can you do, right? Pays the goddamn bills.

College kids trickle in and out asking me useless questions about the professors, schedules, how to enroll for classes. All the shit you can find on the Internet. You can even diagnose yourself. I still wonder why they needed to ask so many questions, though I never liked people to begin with. Just wanted to do my job. Earn my dope and shove off.

My boss insists on having a television for the lobby. I turn on the news and I see a house on fire. *I see a house on fire.* I. See. A. House. On. Fire.

It is my house. My Nick.

My boss does not let me leave, says she'll fire me if I step out to save my own fuckin' life. I tell her to take the job and shove it up her cunt, gather my things and walk out. You don't come between a person and their life. It's just not ethical. She was not ethical.

I'm at my home now, standing outside on the lawn as sirens and chaos try to put out the flames. I am crying at this point. I don't know what to think. Who knows what to think? Who has information? I slowly realize that it wouldn't do me any good. Blurbs written in the dark, that's all these witnesses can give me. I try to pray, but I forget I'm not religious enough for hope.

They're bringing a body out now. Though my vision is smeared I can see it's him. I feel as if the walls of my flesh collapse. I want to die with him, I want this fur to melt off of me as they wheel his body closer. I grab the hand of his charred remains and I feel it is him. They get his identity while I drape my tears over what is left.

Every night I dream about this, and I still cannot wake myself up.

I'm at the trial now. Police investigators have found the man who started the fire. They said he had a beef with Nick, that Nick ran too far away from this man, and then this man had to rip him out of my world. That's what he does. His name is Lorenzo. He tries to steal what he wants from you, and when he cannot have it, he destroys it. I watch them put this wolf on trial, steel fur lingering over his body. The motherfucker is not worried at all. I fear he will be let go. That is our justice system. Let the real bad folks go because they can buy the good lawyers. The scumdog's best fuckin' friend. I know Lorenzo. I used to be a customer—

I wake up finally, turn over to meet the little lab mouse that keeps his peace. I know we are not supposed to be attached to each other, but I cannot help it tonight. I need a warm body to keep the ghosts from coming in.

Look at this. You can't even fuckin' imagine the shit that goes on in the world. Angel Death's got her hands sprawled across the goddamn globe as we trickle through perfect families and piss-poor workweek problems of the First World, but we're all junkies of some sort. Sex addicts, potheads, shopaholics, alcoholics, you fuckin' name it and there's a disorder on it. The whiff of the Acacian dream. But we all want that, want that better life we're entitled to after overworking our fragile bones, too goddamn tired to really hold our lovers at night. I'm merely a part of it, a humble servant to the goddess of money, and fuck Christ, do I work myself just to see those paper tits fly into my fuckin' wallet. She buys you everything, gets you the new addiction to pump through your body; she feeds you and keeps you housed. Shit, she even gets you a girlfriend or two, or in my personal case, a tight little boyfriend. She got me my car, but when she left me, they started to threaten to take my wheels away. So I paid them with what little I had, but the bill collectors don't wait, man. They sift and suck through your wallet and bank accounts until it's time to call it quits, and they're callin' it quits today.

The sun is barely shining through the clouds this morning as their trucks are beeping backwards onto my driveway. It's the repo-dudes, come to take my only transportation, but what does it matter? I couldn't pay for it anyways, the goddess has forsaken me in my rough times, just like the other gods forsake their followers because there's just so many of us. So goddamn many of us, praying to 'em, cloggin' up their fuckin' message queue with no time to deliver results.

It's why I've hated religion, it's a luxury I cannot afford. Just hearing these bastards sink their hooks onto the car makes my spots burn, makes the need for a cigarette all that more intense. I open the drawer and grab a pack of cigs, my computer screen glaring at me as I continue to watch the degenerate slobs conduct their disorderly business on my fuckin' driveway. But it's all soothed out as a cool puff of nicotine slides its way through my body. My fur loosens up for a small moment as I take in a few more life-threatening puffs. I know I'm going to die one day; we're all too focused on that. On dying. We've forgotten what it's like to really live, being responsible and buying funerals before we're in the goddamn ground. Life insurance, salads, banking institutions, the fuckin' list goes on as we work to purchase our perfect send off into the afterlife. We've really forgotten what it feels like to dream; only remember that the real expression of yourself is a fuckin' country song on the radio by doped up cash-cow wannabes; bulls with neatly trimmed horns for good images on the forgotten CD covers. Like you know what a fuckin' CD is.

It ain't even started my day yet and this is what I got to wake up to, bunch of fuckin' assholes taking away my means to get to work. These fuckin' people, scum of the goddamn earth they are. They don't understand what real living is about, what it means to dig far beneath your skin to find answers to the wicked sensations of the world. They only know paychecks because lady money is paying them too much attention. And that's to be expected, fuckin' slumlords of the universe get all the glory when the honest folk get shat on by the rest of the flying debris that lands on our laps. And so it goes.

Tires screech against pavement as I pour myself a scotch over ice. Today's not a work day apparently, and I'm not going to bother with the hassle of acquiring backup vehicles when the loan persons deem it fit to prevent me from workin'. And I know what you're saying, "Why the fuck didn't you just pay the bill?" You think it's easy, don't you? You pay the bills for so goddamn long and never get behind only to have a fuckin' tragedy happen to ya. It forces you to cut corners and cut bills while your account drains slowly, like squeezing the juice of a tomato. You don't know life, sadly, you probably never will. You'll only know what you have planned. You'll never know what the universe has floating around, what useless pocket of disaster is waiting to pour its steaming pile of garbage over you. You plan for everything, well, good for you.

It's not that easy when you're poor. Working two or three jobs just ain't what you want it to be. The piss-poor cash earned from them all barely add up to rent some months. As it stands right now, there's just no place for a decent minimum wage, as much as we would enjoy that. See, the sanity of logic in politics is something we as citizens never get to see, but it would be highly beneficial to the working folk like myself who are constantly getting evicted and repoed. I guess we all need to be reminded of our own insignificance at times. It is what it is.

The sound of the shower starts to blast from the bathroom. It appears my personal friend is finally awake as I hear him scuffling about. Some things are better to go through with company—misery is only part of the handful of diseases that like to be among groups of more than one person. Before I could go and grab my little boy toy, the repo-bastards knock on my door. Burying the remainder of my cigarette into the ashtray, I go and open up. Unashamed of my presence, I greet them in full nudity, because fuck 'em. They're indecent individuals and I was not going to be decent for them.

"Um…" A large scruffy reptilian stood dumbfounded before me, not sure what to say aside from the imbecile word floating around his mouth. His eyes are fixated around my hips, and though I was not standing at full attention, I wasn't afraid of a little cold air.

"It's a fuckin' penis. I'm sure you've seen a few, now what do you want?" Annoyed, I spit the words at his face in hopes to make the rest of this endeavor go quicker. My fingers slowly tap at the edge of the door as I wait for the fucker to actually speak. His partner, a fairly rounded black bear in stained coveralls that read "J.J.'s Towing" was approaching the situation. But what situation was there, really? I mean, so fuckin' what, I'm standing naked in my doorway. It's my own home and I've every right to do so. Plus, the neighborhood ain't up yet so the children are safe from my standing ovations.

"Um…sir, we'll be needing your keys," the pudgy gecko in front of me finally blurts out as he realizes his backup has finally arrived.

Without a beat, I toss the keys at the swine and tell them I had nothing in the car. After a while of being behind, you learn not to keep anything in your vehicle in case these asswipes should appear at your place of residence.

Shutting the door, I could smell him—wet fur mixing with dollar store soap from the shower. "I know you're behind me, my ears hear your steps drizzling all over my floor," I greet him while turning. He only returns a smirk that I could just smack off of his face, but then that'd make me some kind of wife-beater I'm sure. Even though he's got a penis, his body is rather feminine in its physique. He glistens as the sun finally steps out of the clouds and shines over us, seeping through the window and making his shadow larger than his fuckin' ego.

"You gonna fuck me with that thing or just use it to insult the vagrants takin' your car?" he teases gently. I know he is teasing me because I don't pay him to fuck, just pay him for his time. "D, the extra time's gonna cost if I'm not outta here by eight." He takes his towel and dries the rest of himself off.

Every other movie or story has it where a guy doesn't use a hooker for sex, just needs someone to talk to. I'm no different, but I'm not the same as those guys either. They're the stand-up citizens, moral enough to treat their time like a confessional, only they're not in a box, just a room going over the same motions. Actions are religious. It's second nature to nearly everyone. The confessee prays, *Bless me, father for I have sinned, for I have wasted myself again*, and the little bitch touches your arm and tells you it's gonna be okay because you're a good person. We're all good people at times, we all understand what it feels like to be nice; it's just that some of us can't conform. At the end of your time, you set out the cash, maybe smoke a cigarette, and watch them leave. You'll call them again. We all have sins hidden. We all have something we need to confess.

"Your money's on the table, maybe next time I'll gather the drive to pound that little ass of yours," I tease back. I'm not a decent person, I don't use him for my confessions and there ain't a priest in the world that wants to hear them. I haven't done anything wrong in my life, but goddamn have I thought of it. It's what makes us all who we are, the difference between fuckin' animals and citizens. We all make that choice and each time I bring this guy into my home, I choose to sit him down, pour him a drink, and maybe sleep with a warm body next to me. Do I want to fuck him? Yeah, I do. I mean, look at him. Fit fuckin' twink, who wouldn't wanna tap that ass? Maybe I will one day, who knows, right? But for now, I give him his money and send him on his merry fuckin' way so I can handle the thought of getting my car back after the fuckin' collectors have been bustin' my balls every which way but the right way. I may call him again tonight, I ain't worried about the cash, here today, gone in an hour, it doesn't fuckin' matter anymore. Money's just something you have and then it goes away. Like love, you got it, then it leaves ya. Maybe it returns, maybe it doesn't. Hard to say what the universe has in store for us, folks.

The sun is just the right amount of bright this morning. It looks over us all as we move through our constant fuck-ups and senseless degenerative actions. You got to wonder how it bears it up there. I mean, I haven't even made it to forty yet and I'm already sick of hearing what we do wrong on the news every day. The stress of everyone else's lives turns my fur stiff, but I've grown a little apathetic to people. And why not? We've all got our own problems. I know I have mine that I'm not sharing with anybody at the moment, otherwise I'd be in a different situation. I don't even want to know what Nick would say if he saw this. So I pour another tall glass of scotch and down it like a desperate alcoholic. But I'm not addicted to alcohol. I'm addicted to noise and I've been living in silence ever since he died. My house is filled with quiet decadence, that soothing sensation of silence that allows for the mind to wander and concentrate, only I don't want that. I want to remain grounded, but I can't get there. Not as I am, a broke man living without his scent lingering around. No, this isn't living, it's just being here, and the realization bleeds in all too well. If I could unzip my veins, I'd pull them out, but you can't pull out the truth from your own goddamn body. They have to take it from you. They, the degenerates walking the streets. They, the people who move on without thinking of yesterday, who literally forget how we fuckin' came about. How the livid Sky God puked us up onto this world to take away the only ones who made life worth something. But this feeling is universal. I'm not the only one with it, I'm aware of this. I'm aware of how many people go through this depression and how easy it is to get out of it and to fall back into it. This is my addiction. The abyss is my addiction. Should it be my addiction is a question that I cannot force myself to answer because the feeling keeps the wood-colored splotches along my fur from burning. Birthmarks can seem like boils to anyone, but Dalmatians have to feel out of place from the rest of these normal civilians.

You can't get rid of this feeling; you can kill it for a few hours like you murder a headache with aspirin and alcohol, but you can never get rid of it. Slowly, you depend on it like breathing or else you die. That's how it is with addiction. There's no real escape; there's running. Lots of running away and leaving it behind you, but it's never a guarantee that you're strong enough to remain in the past. You drop back into the abyss eventually, get up and try again; only it's harder to kick. We all have our own ways of killing our addictions; I've had mine for a little while now. Weary hands clutch at the air until they grab the cheap little plastic. My vision is only slightly blurry as I slide my thumb across the screen and begin dialing the number for my frequent companion. I've never gotten his name, been seeing him for a year. I just know he hooks up with guys and we all pay him. The others probably get their little fucks here and there, and that's okay. Sex is just sex in a way. Get your frustration out in a few wanks and shots, maybe you even spill it on the kid's face and that's hot for you. Who cares? I never ask him about his other clients, not that it's any of my business.

"Hello?"

I can hear his voice is a little leery. I've never called him this early in the day before. I've never called him right after he has left before, but I don't feel comfortable being alone. It's mostly a night job for him, but I'm falling hard into the abyss.

"I need you to come back," is all I'm able to utter into the phone. My voice is shaky from the anxiety running through my arms. I can feel the quaking murmur of loneliness flushing out of my chest, goddamn it feels right. Though I'm tempted to hang up the phone, I stay with him. There's a second of silence, uncertainty in the air. I can't even begin to imagine what he's thinking about me at the moment.

"D, you know I got other clients today!" His voice was indignant, but I can understand. When you're called on by several guys and perverts, you have to ensure your own safety, and though I'm not unstable, he will never know that. He will only see my shakiness, my uneasiness; aspects of a fuckin' junkie. And maybe I am one, it's not something I'm concerned with at the moment. If these little nicks in our conversation present any form of uncertainty in his own life, he's not going to answer. I try to calm myself, slowly. I take in a few heavy breaths, light a cigarette before providing my next answer.

"It's happening again."

Composure remains firm between my words, whether it persuades him is another matter that I hope I won't have to deal with. Despite wanting to fall back into this addiction, it's not something I want to remain in. Parts of me understand that there are other aspects of life that you can cling to; the past isn't always something to hold. And you shouldn't always live there, even if you feel you left yourself there. I'm still there at the fire watching them pull his wrecked corpse from the broken glass with ashes littered around, but I need to live with time. *He* helps me live. Little lab mouse, I don't even know his fuckin' name, yet I've been calling him, bringing him into my home so to keep the thoughts of some dead guy in the past. He is my desperation at nights, the embodiment of my weakness, of how far into the abyss I keep descending to. There's a tragedy inside us all and he's taken the brunt of the whole production since I've lived here. Letting out an immense sigh, the phone starts to tremble in my palm. There's a stigmata there, on both palms really. It bleeds through to the back of my hand, and it burns the most when I think of how much weight it is to heal when you don't want to.

"You're growing attached, D. This is the third time this week you've called me. It's starting to scare me a little. I don't think I can pull you out this time..." His words linger between networks as my breath crumbles through my teeth. My body does not have the strength to say anything further, so I hang up the call and drape myself at my desk. Staring outward into the neighborhood, I feel Nick slowly press against me. I've left the embers behind. I don't know what happened to the rubble of our last home. I never felt the need to look it up. I simply left for here, a dingy elderly suburb that will one-day turn into some ghetto because everyone here is apathetic to the presence of a neighborhood. Still he followed. I never escaped him, and I don't know if I wanted to escape him. I want to function, but I am unsure what it means to function. This is what ghosts do, they haunt you. He's just one I cannot let go. And so it goes.

I remember when they lowered him into the ground. Closed casket. No one should have to see the deceased charred and left unknown. My hand rested on the box as the family said their peace. I had to remain calm, kept breathing, couldn't let the tears come out. I couldn't cry. Men don't cry. My parents taught me that.

As they put the body to rest, the rain began to spill over us. I always thought of it as the earth watering our corpses when we die, much like we water plants when we place them in the ground. We return ourselves. This is our circle. We're born, live in debt for most of our lives and die off. We get lowered into the dirt and the rain comes. Maybe when the time passes, flowers will grow.

Rental cars are another disgusting scam that we pay for. You walk in there and go to pick up your car only to find out they tack on extra charges for extra insurance, GPS navigation, and other frivolous bullshit. I mean, how many people have a fuckin' cell phone nowadays? It's how we track people in this country, yet they still fill the need to sell me a fuckin' GPS with a rental.

Acacia is one big tracking field, one of the few countries where you know the exact movements of the guy across the street because of his phone blasting it to the satellites, storing our information in the sky. Free country, my fuckin' ass. We're free in the sense that I can shoot the next guy I see because he was looking at me funny. And I can get away with it just by claiming that I stood my ground to not let vicious creatures take advantage of me. But that's how this country works. Acacia, land of many promises and poor people. People who can afford to let their kids die from a gun and say it was an accident. But they never are; it's simply neglect. And that's only a portion of the problem.

I got my rental car today so I can go to work like a normal being on this planet. It was hard finding work after

Nick died, but I found some gig giving students financial aid for college—one of the largest scams we have as a nation.

A man can only take enough vacation days before they start rolling you back in with phone calls and text messages about what you haven't finished yet; what was left on your desk before you left last Friday, fuckin' calling you, pissed off because you're out of the office and have been for the past few days. I suppose job loss threats can get you out of any goddamn rut and into a fuckin' suit and tie. I got an office of my own, fortunately. The lights are too bright so I keep them off and use the sunlight from the window instead. Downing half a bottle of aspirin, I flip on the computer and start processing the timesheets left on my desk. Fuckin' government work programs for students, great idea for them, I suppose. Let any fuckin' student come in and get a job, and believe me, we got some crazy-ass fuckers here. Most of these people I wouldn't have given a job because of how indignant they get with you, but it ain't up to me. I just got handed these people from the last person when I inherited this job. It's an easy gig at times, just approve and post, approve and post, and then HR does the rest.

My cell's been vibrating like crazy lately. It's the kid, the little lab mouse bugging me over and over. I haven't called him since the last interference I had and he left me there. I don't know if I'm mad, but I figure I'd give him some space and let him handle his other clients until I need him again. That's all he's there for anyways, companionship when you need it; when it's convenient for it. Maybe it's a little childish not to respond to him, but I'm a busy guy, I can't deal with every person in my life, which isn't anyone in particular, I suppose. I mean, fuck, one person is a lot for me to handle being an introverted asshole 90 percent of the time. Anyways, the kid's been bugging my phone. It's not normal for him to seek me out. He said I was getting too attached to him, so I've been hiding my phone to avoid the temptation of calling.

I want to see him again. Ely is holy to me, but I can't let him know that. I can't let him know that I want to break the client relationship we hold. My ghosts won't let me. Neither will Ely. All around it's a bad situation. I lose him, but I don't really know if he would want me. Ely can handle me now that I'm a client, but breaking that would change us. He's nineteen and I'm like fifteen years older than him. Although it sounds perfect, the fuckin' societal norms seem to think otherwise. But what are the societal norm anyways?

I continue to ignore my phone. It's only filled with messages of "haven't seen you in a while," and "when are you going to call me, I miss you." Horseshit statements I'm sure that are given to everyone else. He misses being paid, that's all the world is ever about. We're a society of business ethics, even when it comes to our friendships. Who can we benefit from, who can pull us out of the fuckin' grime when we need it? Keep these scums close in case we get put in a bad spot, because you will one day. You'll get so far deep that you're going to be begging people to pull you out. You always do. I always do, only I can't beg people anymore. I've lost that; I don't even know where my friends are. Years of alienation do that to people, I suppose. Then again, there are still folks on the lower side of the world I can shake hands with; broken doctors performing alleyway abortions in a germ-infested bathroom because the Acacia laws are too conservative to believe that women actually get raped. That's the problem with the "decent" folk of this world. They don't see what it really is to live through tragedy, they blame victims and feel sympathy for the guy or gal who did the fuckin' crime. We're misguided, heavily, by unorthodox sky gods that don't ever talk to us. We simply have to speak through them, and there comes a time when you gotta really dig deep into your firm beliefs and wonder if this is what your god would have wanted. Have you forgotten them? Do you really know them like you thought? When's the last time you took them out for dinner?

You need friends like that. You need those who can do the dirty work because there's no fuckin' way everyone is clean in this world. There are just things we simply cannot do that they can. It's the end if you need to call them.

I'm processing these time sheets, ensuring that these little fuckers are going to their job on time and making sure they're not in there during their scheduled classes because fuck Christ, it's my ass if they're working when they're supposed to be going to class. That's not how this program was designed, they need to study more than they need to work, but I get it. I understand being broke, I can empathize with those people. Empathy isn't a skill I know well. If anything, I'm apathetic to most students at this university, and though some have real problems, there isn't always ways to get around Big Brother's way of tearing out your asshole.

There's an argument going around that higher education should be free. We're piling loans on our future and creating indentured servants forced to work for wages that barely work for living expenses. Marriage isn't even a thing anymore because who can afford it? I'm sorry, babe, I have $138,000 of student loans I gotta pay, I can't afford our $50,000 wedding. The conservatives blame sex; well fuck 'em. They call it hook-up culture. All the young folk want to fuck. They don't understand the values of relationships. Sex isn't the problem here, it's the financial strain being put on the students. I'll say, it's hard to believe that higher education should be free because I worked a couple jobs while going to school without my fuckin' parents spending a dime. Don't even know where those people are at, and I don't intend to search for them.

Education is one big lie. I can't say it's the worst mistake anyone could make, but it's certainly not the messiah that's going to save the country. Until that bubble pops, we're stuck in a cycle of enlarging debt, and it's going to hurt when it finally crashes. And it will one day; I can only hope I'm alive to see it happen when it does.

There's loud noises booming outside of my office; the sounds of an angry customer screechin' their words through their teeth because of something they don't agree with. I can see her, black-furred feline clawing the newly furnished desks of our customer service reps up front as she shouts her disgust. People like her sicken me sometimes. There's a fuckin' voting process. You don't like the federal guidelines, then go write your fuckin' congressmen. But they don't understand that, and they don't want to understand that. They're like rest of the general public, stupid and misinformed; force-fed dreams of making a better life for yourself and feeling entitled to take what you feel is owed to you. Well, Acacian law doesn't work that way, lady. I can hear her getting louder and louder; this goddamn office holding her echoes like a music box ready to fuckin' blow. I'm staring at her and all I can wonder is how the fuck she left her house with her drug-addicted face all busted up with bright-ass makeup. I mean, she looks like a fuckin' clown. I can't even keep a straight face, but I'm going to have to. The lady's getting angrier and angrier by the moment, so I get up and close my door to keep the noise from killing my ears. It must have given the bitch a sign because she quieted down quick. Right now her name's on a list of people she don't want to be on. When we know your name and know your voice, you've been an insanely troublesome person for us and we're not giving you any decent treatment.

My phone's vibrating again. It feels like I'm not going to get any fuckin' work done today, so I grab it and answer the goddamn call. "Yes?" is all I say, disgruntled and waiting for good answer.

"Hey D, haven't heard from you in a while. Thought I'd call to see if you needed any company tonight." His words playfully trudge through the phone's speaker, but there's a sense of fear in them. I wonder if he had a bad john—if someone roughed him up. I don't pay too much attention to it though. These days aggravation can make a dude do terrible things. At least in my case, but that's how it's always been, make the wrong decisions due to your own anger and bullshit. It's what makes life drop you a few floors down. I've turned away from my computer screen to stare outside for a moment. It's gray out there, dismal, though I love it. There's a certain peace inside the graying of nature. That lady is still screaming her head off out there, but it's not my concern anymore. I've shut her out since I closed the door. You close out distractions one after another.

"Hey, um," I start calmly. I don't intend to mess this thing up that we have; this little relationship that's been buzzing between us—nights of deranged discussions and harsh wails ending with broken alcohol bottles and wasted scotch. He's taken the brunt of a lot of things within my walls, and though I pay him money, it doesn't mean he's not special. There's not a whore out there that could take what I've been giving out to him. If only I could love, I wonder what that would look like. "Listen, I don't think tonight's a good night. My back's been beating me something fierce lately, leavin' me tired. Don't think I'll be up for company."

"You know, I've been a little concerned about ya. You been all right?" Calamity-clacking words are wrangling around in my skull. My moods have been rather pissed off lately, and it's taking almost every fuckin' muscle to keep from pissing him off. What can I say though?

"I'm all right, like I said, just been tired lately. I'll call you sometime." There's a disappointing sigh lingering in his throat. I can't tell you if he really wanted to see me or not, I like to think that he does, though. It makes the money all that less meaningful to me. I don't wait for an answer. My thumbs simply slide across the touchscreen of my phone and end the call.

I stopped worrying about the eeriness of silence after Nick passed. After some time, you start to get used to it, and though I have had many nights where I was not alone, I still understand the silence that lingers around my home. It's like addiction, there's no getting rid of it, only running away from it. Turn the television sound up, play music, what the fuck ever to keep it from creeping in, but it don't work that way. It'll always be there. It grows on you.

Days at work are always the same, get in around eight in the morning and get bitched at all day by self-entitled assholes who think it's their job to make you miserable. Like that lady screaming about something she probably don't even understand. Most of them don't, but that's just how they live, in the dark with a broken flashlight called television. Media is important when it's not bought out by the corporate whack jobs and politicians selling our rights away. I wonder how much I'm worth?

It'll be like this tomorrow and the next day and fuck would I hate it if it didn't pay the bills. And it does, thankfully, aside from a few that just ain't happening right now, but you work it out. There's nothing else you can do but work it out. Show the situation your teeth and let it know you ain't going to get scared off so fuckin' easily. It gets easier that way.

I got some vegetables sizzling in the pan in some oil, television blaring the news about another Amber Alert. Poor kid. You wish their lives were easier, and move on. Most of us who get those alerts on our phones don't bother taking note at our surroundings. Those cars might have passed me five, six times before and I wouldn't have noticed. We're desensitized to what a real crisis is. If we ever get nuked, we won't know what to do, aside from force Jesus down the throats of all the non-believers. But for now it's neither here nor there. That's just our country, protected, spoiled, and entitled. The rest of the world knows it.

These vegetables are frying up nicely, though I don't have a clue as to what I'm really going to cook them with. I usually never do until I dance around the fuckin' kitchen with burning greens on the stove. I open up my fridge and start to rummage around until a knock splatters on my door. I don't even know who would want to visit me at this fuckin' time but I'm not in the mood to be sold to Jesus. I know how those fuckin' Jehovah's Witnesses work and the Mormons. Same fuckin' concept all around. One time, I had a nun come up and try to sell me cookies. So I gave her some money. What was I supposed to do, turn down a little old lady selling cookies? She's a fuckin' nun. I may not believe in her god, but I always have time for cookies. It's like turning down those fuckin' kid troops. You just don't do it. Unless you're diabetic. Then you can do it respectfully, with a lot of emphasis on that last word there.

That knock is splattering all across my door, like a dude getting boned hard against the wall, only without the moans. I turn down the greens and take out a pack of chicken from the fridge. I don't even look out the little hole to see who it is. The door swings open and all I can say is, "What?" Indignant words linger as I'm taken aback. The concerned little hooker come to bother the John.

The sun is still hanging above us though slowly declining as the late hours are setting in. Summers always have a late evening; there are days where it's rather nice. My eyes look him over from his feet to his head, nervousness in his body, uncertainty in his face; he is afraid of me. Saying nothing else, I step aside and motion for him to wander into my home, the greens probably burning by now, but I'm not concerned about that anymore.

"We talked earlier." I let the words linger about the air like cigarette smoke. There wasn't much more to say from that really. We did discuss the minor absence between us, and yet he is standing here, in my home.

"I know, but I needed to talk with ya. I was hoping you'd call me over for a night, but you've been a little distant lately since our last full night together." His fur is stiff as he lets the words drip carelessly from his mouth. Heavy, they fall into the floor leaving invisible indentions in each wooden panel. As he talks, I walk over to my kitchen and take the food off the stove. I don't believe I'll be eating tonight. "Listen," he continues, tongue trembling to get the words beyond his lips, "I'm getting out of the business. My clients won't be able to call me anymore."

I never thought he'd actually leave it. He's young enough though, there's still years of life he has yet to experience. "What's making you tremble right now?" I ask flatly.

"Well, you see, some of my other clients haven't been too happy with that."

"I can see why, with a body like yours." I'm only being honest with him. "I take it a couple hurt you?" This isn't any of my business, but I'm a curious creature. I don't see the bruises, but I'm sure there's a few hiding there underneath his fur. Physical pain is easy to mask, but the emotional scars it leaves will never leave your face. It will out you, whether you want it to or not. He doesn't say anything. The silence almost confirms it. I pull out my wallet and see the usual fee hidden beneath my license. The money wrangles with my fingers as I walk up to him, dropping the neatly folded bits of paper onto the marble countertop. Without much warning, I pull him in for a hug, one last little bit of contact before we part ways. "I'm not asking you to stay, the money's yours. Come back sometime." His hand quakes a little bit before it slightly rubs along my back. He grabs the money and makes his way for the door, the sun beaming through, his body shadowed by its light.

This is all a part of living. People wander around the space of our lives and leave abruptly. Sometimes, the typewriter archiving our past doesn't know how to describe the emptiness the body suffers when the good ones leave. It's why some of us forget who they are; get angry and block them out. We're selfish creatures that way. It's why the world is a childish being waddling around the universe. I suppose if the aliens were watching us, they would probably laugh in understanding at our growing pains. Pains that are near impossible for us to understand right now. Maybe one day our brains will expand far enough. For now, we'll simply shuffle about like vagabonds learning from each other.

In some ways, I already miss him. I don't know where he'll go in his life, but I hope the place is better than where he was. I couldn't imagine the things he had to do for his other clients, and by the fear of his body, I assume it wasn't a pleasant meeting when he told the others. I'm sure they feel entitled to him since he was their little fuck toy, but you're not entitled to anyone. We're free creatures in this place; you can't just walk up to somebody and say I own you. I mean, you could, but that doesn't make it right. Some of Ely's clients were probably dicks. I'm happy for him, at least. I go back to cooking, stomach churning in hunger as I hope the little lab mouse remains a memory and not a haunting.

Superstores are the heartbreak of our country, but we can't get away from them. They're squeezin' our balls with low prices and trading up real jobs for real people with self-checkout and other automated processes. Being a culture of business, everything in our life has to be automated. Get in, get out, too goddamn fast to really know what's going on. There's no time to think, only time to "act now" because of the flashing yellow lights in front of the big blue background. And that's normal to us all, just like it's normal for a ten-year-old in another country to spend sleepless hours making a fuckin' shoe for the middle class. But I'm not focused on the world's problems, I'm just as hypocritical as the next person. Only difference is I don't call myself a patriot like the others do. You shouldn't do that; you shouldn't do it because it just shows your ignorance. That's not a pretty sight.

It's been about two weeks since I've seen him or heard from him. Every so often Ely wanders his way into my skull and I'll dream about him, but nothing more comes of it. It's all part of the process I'm sure; learning how to move on, to forget. It's what we teach ourselves in order to live. We can't be left behind while the world keeps moving forward. Time is that little bitch that doesn't want to slow down, just wants to continue forward while some us want to remain in the moment for a little bit longer. I suppose Ely has moved on too. The kid's tough; he has to be in order to maintain himself.

I'm moving along these aisles, grabbing food for the week, which'll probably last a month because I haven't eaten. Since he left, I haven't felt the need to. My teeth aren't aching to chew up anything, and my tongue doesn't want to taste anything anymore. I can't say for how long, and I'm not too concerned with it anyway. I've stopped sleeping some nights. People can see it in my eyes. My coworkers ask me questions of my home situation and I tell them I'm fine. And I am fine, I'm more than fine, I'm learning how to live all over again. There's transition that happens, and I'm only in that phase until I figure out what I need to do to stay sane because there's so much about myself I could kill. Ely took care of that before he left, now it's up to me to be a big boy and do it myself. This is my strength being tested and there ain't a ghost in the world that's going to fuck it up now. Not when there's so much progress that's been made. The Christians would tell me that God is testing me. It's the same with any other religion, honestly. Tests just happen like that, there's no god involved with it and there shouldn't be. It's not the sky god's prerogative to ensure that you, his humbly living servant, will serve him absolutely. Not when he hasn't talked in like, ever. No, it's your job to see it through. That's what I'm doing, seeing it through.

The store is cluttered with the kind of people you make nice faces to in hopes they move out of your way. My cart's almost full with stuff I probably won't need but want anyway because I only keep up with the façade of grocery shopping. Vegetables? Sure. Fruit? You know it. Junk food? It's what my stomach is made out of. Slowly I start to turn from shopping to people watching because I'm that dude that likes to stare at the tragedy some people carry on their faces. You can tell how hard a person has lived just by the amount of stress weighing down their cheeks. As if gravity is just pulling them closer to the ground because their life is filled with unwanted drama and bullshit. Couples discussing what they're having for dinner hide their troubles within their words. People around won't think any more of the conversation if food is masking it. Food is a wonderful distraction.

Most don't know what they're wearing on their faces. They don't know the secrets dripping from their eyes, how sullen they've become. The public is not a place of solemnity, yet we wander into it for safety from the monsters in our own homes. Monsters that are ready to sell off our bodies into a new world of legitimized slavery. In the end, there's a new drug inside us all, processed, plastic-wrapped, and force-fed to us. And we believe it's all right because why would our dear leaders lie to little old me? Fuck 'em. People have that innate feeling to lie; I'm no different.

The poets are the better people watchers, capturing waves of energy from the various faces, using language to bring out the digested filth these folks have been living in. There are no faces among these people, only suffering, even behind their smiles, there's a hint of their disasters wafting about. It is who we are and what generally keeps us waking up because we are prideful. Our struggles match the wisdom we feel is required to share with the rest of our community, though it's no different than the next person's. We're too similar to each other, too like-minded to truly explore this land we have been so graciously given by whatever god or goddess that looms around out there. And there's something out there, you can feel it in the air, the way it breathes as you buy your fuckin' groceries. You know you're being watched, not by anything natural here, but by something a lot bigger than we could ever understand. Maybe we'll evolve to understand, but that's another matter.

I'm tossing my stuff onto the conveyer belt and the dude's ringing it up. Cute teen, fuckin' mutt. We're all mutts in a way, there's no such thing as being pure anymore. Either way, he's a nice piece of ass, and I can say that because I'm comfortable judging people on their looks. This country's way too restrictive on their views of sex. They don't understand that the reason we're oversexualizing things is because of the conservatives tearing us down. Sex is bad, sex will put you in hell. You'll get STDs, condoms shrivel your penises. I mean this shit goes on and on. All fuckin' day, all over the fuckin' television. Just shut the fuck up and screw already. You know they're repressed and they're miserable, so they take it out on us—the goddamn honest people. Not saying the religious right isn't honest, but you know some senator voted down a gay marriage bill, then sent dick picks to some dude on a hookup site. It's like that all over this goddamn place.

This cashier is going so fuckin' slow, so I got all the time I need to look him up and down. Thick little dude, but a little tummy ain't so bad. My eyes travel along his soft brown arms, noticing there ain't no shag on him. The beeping of his little register is so fuckin' monotonous, almost worthy of a makeshift hypnotherapy session. One little blip after the other, arms trudging back and forth with items, this kid's really holding up the line here.

There's a strange scent in the air now. I know this one, I've smelt it before. The smell itself is distant, but so fuckin' close to me. Eyes slink around people to find the source of this odor. It's something living, breathing; my nostrils are burning as they stretch farther away from me in search of whatever it is in the air. The distance grows stronger, as if it's traveling towards me. Jesus fuck, what is this? Who is this? It ain't the lab mouse, I'd know him instantly. He always smelled like the rain in winter, but this is more like old books and old spice blended and puked onto someone's fur. Nick used to wear that shit; Howl is what they called it. Got you all the girls. They showed it on television; over sexualized beasts trying to manhandle the hot dudes in the shower. Goddamn those dudes were hot too. But I'm losing the point, it's familiar in here. It's Howl, I know it.

There's a man wandering toward the door, fall-tinted fur covered by some glossy jacket, black shine against fluorescent lights, he doesn't want to be seen. He's the one wearing Howl, I smell the fuckin' stench on him. I always hated it. You could get better cologne from the toilet than you could with that horseshit company. They were lucky they had models, otherwise people would boycott that shit. He seemed like an ordinary fox, same auburn color as the next guy, slim-flab dude just meandering his way across the linoleum and through the half-broken automatic doors. I give the cashier my card to pay for whatever the hell I bought as I'm staring at the guy. The kid at the register is probably thinkin' I'm a perv. Well, he's partially right. I was thinking about tappin' his ass earlier, but the fuckin' smell of Howl distracted me. Fuckin' cock blockin' piece of shit.

I'm still staring at this guy and before I decide to leave him alone, I notice his tail; the half-black, half-white tipped appendage swayed fluently left and right, and though I could not see his face, I knew who it was. It freaked me out; hands shook violently as I grabbed my shit and my card and rushed out the door. His fuckin' tail still drawing me in closer. I hoped to one day be rid of these little daylight nightmares, but for now I have to go with the flow.

Usually my episodes are short in public. It's sort of like a short burst of inspiration, only with your past there to hold you back. But nah, this fucker is staying with me. He doesn't dissipate as he moves through the doors. Nick, demon of my past, snatched up by angel death all too swiftly. Such heavenly labyrinths that lay between your fur, how I miss exploring them, but fire purges even the purest of people in this world. Martyrdom in your eyes, you were the persuasion that kept me waking in the morning. Now I wander disgusting supermarkets grabbing things that only keep me alive temporarily.

Lost is your spirit, disgruntled is my body, but he was mercy, wasn't he? Before Ely left, he was the mercy from all of this. The last bit of freedom I could experience without you. Now he is gone, much like you are, and me, I sit here in the present wondering what my life is going to do tomorrow. I am on autopilot because I am not strong enough to move forward, though I have the desire. Why are you here, demon? Why are you walking the market today? What visions drove you mad enough to possess the work in progress that is my sanity? I confess only to you, heavenly demon. There is no god worthy enough to absolve me of the sins that lay about my skull. Fuck, how I penned these monsters into you some nights. You had doors painted with your blood. I opened them and inked out every disgusting little thing I had dreamed or actually took action on. Am I that distasteful to you now? Is your ghost my personal punishment for being a person? Such awakenings are difficult to expose yourself to. I still love you, heavenly demon, and I'm slowly starting to believe that I've grown more than attached to you confessor. But that's love, ain't it? You can't fuckin' keep it, you have to play it as it lays and let it roam where it wants to. You hope it'll come back but you don't hold your fuckin' breath, because you lean more on the disaster than the pretty picture of its return. But you, demon, are not the disaster here. The world snatched your bones away before you could become one in my life. Ely isn't the disaster either, little lab mouse left too early to see what destruction looks like in a person. Underneath all the holiness of your light, demon, I am your disaster, I am Ely's disaster because I cannot let either of you go. I simply loom about what little ashes you both have left me with; remnants of my eyes, how they burn as they sink deeper into the quicksand of the past.

Ghosts understand how to torture a person. It's what they do, what they are designed to do. Their fingers latch onto the person until they feel they are satisfied with their task, but that never happens. Ghosts are hungry creatures, feeding off the fear and suffering of the person they are haunting. It's what they desire most because they're spiteful things. They are also the remembrance we cannot handle ourselves.

I get my stuff packed into the cart. I tell the cashier to have a good day since he's going to have a shitty one anyway. Customer service is the worst job you could ever have because people are generally self-entitled assholes. And they show it all the time. You serve them, and they make sure you know it. Decent individuals are rare and few. Lightly jogging, my eyes are buzzing around the parking lot as I make my way to my rental. Still need to fix the repo issue, but it doesn't matter right now. The universe is throwing way too much shit in my face for one day. The demon buys groceries; the demon stocks them in his car. The demon has a fuckin' car, but I cannot be bothered to keep one fuckin' thing in my own physical universe. My hands only burn what is left, and the demon is here to remind me of that. Though I did not set him aflame, he reminds me of my inability to protect him when he needed me most. Nick, victim of my ineptitude. I can only hope Ely doesn't need my help; I could not handle another spirit wandering this plane of existence merely to satisfy the agenda of pulling memories together.

I want to talk with him, the demon. I want to touch him; to pull him back from angel death and bring him home. I want to share a bed with him again, but he is not there. He is simply a figment of my own addiction. I slowly wheel the cart to the receiver, watching him store his groceries, and I smile when I think of all the times Nick would store the bags neatly, obsessive with how they would fit in the trunk. I suppose it's easy to mistake one for another; it's easy to relapse when you want to keep your addiction bottled up in your chest like a hand grenade, waiting for the right moment to explode.

Demon, you continue to crawl from the abyss and consume me like a hit of mescaline. Why am I unable to kick you back? Why am I so drawn to you? Why must I continue to love you?

I am dreaming. The ignorance of sleep has caught me, bound me to this bed so that the inner consciousness may roam, only I don't like looking at that dude. My subconscious is merely another demon to fight off. He is me, only I can't control him. I can't control my own body when he appears.

I don't like the anger in his skies, the bullets that fall from his clouds. Though he is of my own body, he frightens me. He is that part of me I do not want to see, though it has been awhile. This dog, this inner behemoth is hungry, but I cannot guess as to what it wants anymore. I can no longer taste what reaches its teeth; I can only witness what happens beneath the torrential rains when I arrive.

He is in love; we're a lot alike that way. I wonder if he can keep a guy around, unlike my pompous ass. I have never seen the person he is in love with, it could be more than one, but that is not why I am here. Although I live beside him in the same body, we are separate from each other. A consciousness that works to keep from meeting at some point like this. But these meetings happen anyways. We all have to live with a duality in ourselves; a third eye of sorts. We just rarely see it. It's there in your dreams, in the parts where you are asleep, where the inner being of yourself can wander, like now. But that is all part of living in a way. Even though we are alone in our world, we're never truly alone.

The future is not made to be predicted, but I goddamn should have seen this coming when I left that fuckin' store. This is the temple of my slumber, the inner poison that I hide away; the part of me that bashes the keyboard with angry letters through venomous fingertips. The entity of my subconscious is my shepherd in a way, the little bit of myself that won't allow me to destroy things in this world. He sought out the little lab mouse, deranged fuck. That is who we are in a way. We are all mad on this world; mad from life itself, not ready to feel her warm embrace. We can only light the fireworks in hopes to bring down the stars in the skies. We want them on ourselves to remind us that we are not bound by gravity, that we can do absolutely anything we want to. We just haven't figured it out yet.

I am in his world, though there are times when he enters in mine. He has more control than I do; I am not yet ready for that responsibility. My body knows this, it's why he's here. It's why we see each other every so often, and though I know why I'm seeing him tonight, I also know there's damage control to be done. That's been a long time coming, I guess. It's that part of life you just don't want to do, but you have to because if you don't, it ruins you. And you can't be ruined forever.

We stand together in the middle of the road, empty, it's always empty here. I guess he likes it that way. In dreams, almost anything is possible, so he keeps it the way he wants it. It's like me and how I keep my house, empty, but I'm not sure I really want it empty. We all go through those questions in our lives, even the bitter slumber that is myself.

He says nothing, only stares at me as he moves closer. Wet paws trudge through slick roads as I meet his eyes. I remember when I met Ely. I was not in control. It was merely my other doing the driving, the talking, and everything else. I was only the secondary pilot while he took over. It was raining as it is now, exactly like this, little needle bullets falling without grace.

Water splattering onto the dingy city roads as he drove me to some place with broken neon lights and a few infested alleyways; infested with cum and piss and any other fluid that leaves the body on a frequent basis. And though it was raining, the little lab mouse still stood on the sidewalk, waiting for his next customer.

I said nothing as the inner demon made the call; substituted the desire for someone with the availability of a slut. But Ely was more than that; I found that out over the past year. Ely, sweetest manna of all life, I slowly became a slut for you, and though I never offered myself up for sacrifice, the stories buried beneath my ribcage exposed enough of myself for you to know me, to know him, and to know the ashes that trickle in my past. If I could, I would dig my claws into you; I would fuck you, but I cannot allow myself to ruin what mercies fall from the sky. I can always say I knew mercy, truly knew his face, and I can also say that I wish I had him back. But I am merely alone for this time, left with the behemoth in my dreams.

He reaches me and wraps himself around me. He is like weeds, but strong enough to hold the poison out of me. It is his way of telling me that it is time to move on now. It is time to vanquish the ghosts that rattle around my world and move forward. I fear he is no longer strong enough to keep me from my own destruction, but we all have limits. I just reached them all too quickly.

My ghosts drive cars and buy groceries. They know how to fuck passionately like any other living person. They know how to live, and yet there is no living for me. Me, I only know how to look back at them; how to write history books with dead memoirs and broken apologies, but these are my remnants. Little specs that my fingers keep entrapped beneath my fur.

I do not understand what it is to move on, but I live like I do. I eat dinner and go to work, earn cash and pay bills like the rest of the society. My smiles appear genuine, but plastic is simply that deceiving. Would I be empty without my ritualistic noise? Was I empty without the little lab mouse leaving pieces of himself around my home? Though he is now gone, I still get a whiff of his scent on my covers, my couch; something I can no longer get from Nick. Fire washes all traces of yourself from this world. But it is time now. There isn't another one like Ely, and Nick isn't much for talking. He never was. But it's not the prerogative of the ghost to discuss its reasons with you. They're there to make you remember how much of a bastard you are, and apparently I'm a pretty fucked up bastard to keep seeing him, or I'm simply tormenting myself with it all and refuse to let anything go. And that's probably more likely, in all honesty. I mean, it's the classic textbook bullshit that is spewed out, and I somewhat believe in the shit.

The news is coming on now, fuckin' early morning nonsense. They tell you all about the weather and the goddamn traffic that's flooding up our freeways as a buffer between who shot who, who killed who, who raped who. There are tragedies all over this fuckin' world. And we live like it too, there's not an emergency in our hearts that doesn't turn into something tragic later on. There's just not an operator to fix the looming breakage of the mental condition of ourselves. Only we can fight that, and how we do that is everyone's own choice. Most decide to off themselves, and while others believe them to be cowards, I don't agree. It's simply how those individuals chose to handle their own misery. It's not our business to see who it had affected in the aftermath. I almost followed the same path, should have followed it, but here I am now, discussing ways to move forward with living. Wanting to die is all a part of living. It's not an easy process to learn; there's no button to press to make it all easy or to let you know it's going to get better soon.

They're talking about him: the man that ripped my little fox from my arms; the man that charred him up and left his spirit roaming around me. Headline sprawled across the flat-screen, high definition, the letters just booming from the screen. I can hear the blues guitar in my heart wailing somber notes as I read about his release. A fuckin' standard press release, but what can they do?

Lorenzo will move on, maybe I will, maybe I won't. But I know he will, ghosts don't haunt the demoralized. They hang around in hopes to have an effect, but it never happens that way. They're merely ectoplasm in the wind of this dude's carnage. I could kill the bastard. I should kill the bastard. But I won't. I won't because why fuckin' bother? I can't tell if it'd shake the spirits from my life, and he may just become another one. There's simply nothing I can argue logically to make it work. But I can stare at him, his worn fuckin' face, scarred up nose, wrinkles flowing from his brow. He has not aged well. His gray has faded from his fur. The man is like cigarette smoke and ash with yellow eyes—a mere waving existence. So many have been lost inside his eyes. I still find myself losing ground when I look into them. They simply take you. He had the face of business. Smug. Invincible. Yet, not a damn soul is invincible. Karma sees to that. It swiped up my car and the little lab mouse. It stole my Nick. There is no more nectar in my home, there are merely the droplets of what remains, and he sits on that fuckin' screen with his fucked up sense of surviving. But who is anyone to understand survival?

So this fucker is out now. Who knows what he'll do, who he'll hurt next. But that is not my business. I have my own path that I need to move on to. My own problems to fix. He is simply a weed left behind, failing to grow. Some thorns in our past remain stagnant because there is no real need for them to move on with you.

At my desk, I open my work email and fire one off for a vacation. It's my time, I fuckin' earned it and I'm going to use it, goddamn it. Two weeks should be enough to yank the barbwire from my ribcage and finally get the world straight again. Lighting a cigarette, I see the early morning moon dissipating as the sun takes its rightful place. It lingers in the sky, knowing it's going to return in a few hours. In the early stages of our lives, we believed that the moon was the king of darkness, that he would defeat the sun and reign terror among us for the night hours. Then the sun would defeat the moon and all would be right again. Somehow, among all our advancements, we're still there at the beginning. Our minds haven't expanded that far yet. It takes a lifetime for the general brain to grow, and I'm still waiting on mine to expand. Until then I take my Jack and a smoke, and I wait.

When some people are addicted to something, anything, they look to prayer to get them out. They focus on some sky god because you can't fuck with faith. Faith is that rock that sits between everybody's hearts; that little indention that everyone carries about the unknown. It'll always be unknown, but they have to fill that void with something, so they make up a book and shove it down the throats of millions of people. And we're expected to believe it. No questions asked, just roll with it and see what happens. They're saying atheists are waging wars against the other countries on this planet, but I don't see that flag up there when our boots hit the ground of the evildoers along the cold waters where we import the goods of Acacia. But those are merely uninformed politics. Wars are simply more difficult to understand than we'd like to believe. As a society, we're dumbing ourselves down, though we've grown so much.

Acacia, where the media feeds us pure granulated bullshit. It's typical of them, of anyone who lives in the First World. We have all forgotten what it feels like to really think for ourselves, the sky god is coming for us. He is going to save us; he is going to bring us into the light.

But he did not die for my sins. He may have been a martyr for someone out there, it just wasn't me. And I like it that way. That's a debt I could not pay.

Yes, we turn to prayer because where else is there to turn to? We're at the hard bottom of life, trying to dig our way out of the fuckin' abyss, but we're not strong enough. So we tug at the little rock that everybody carries in hopes we can keep ourselves from remaining trapped on the darker side of life. But I don't turn to conventional prayer. There is no amen at the end of my confessions. My prayers are not offered to the god that is so popular here, but to the sexual deviant of Nila, goddess of love, goddess of all things carnal.

It is raining and I'm driving my fuckin' rental down Truth and Navigation, a fuckin' crossroad you don't want to be at in the wrong hours. But it's where I met him; it's where Ely came into my life. It's where I became codependent on his presence; it's where I fell in love for the second time in life. Real fuckin' love, not the grade school valentine card bullshit. Real love, where you find someone and are fulfilled; when they become your nirvana.

The rain is coming down hard. I can barely see the fuckin' street signs, but there's no lights here anymore. The city won't come out and fix them. West side of my town is truly the forgotten. Sometimes, being forgotten is a good thing; get washed out of history, out of life. You may even be able to slowly whisper your presence elsewhere and start anew; how I wish I could start over.

My tires are rolling and thumping constantly; my seats slowly become little massagers to my ass because of the fuckin' cracks and rocks in the road. I hope there ain't no needles to fuck up my tires, but that is merely a gamble I have to take. There ain't no moon out tonight, no stars, just pure black abyss; pure unwanted souls. Am I unwanted? I don't know, but I always feel at home here.

I can see the busted, flickering fluorescence nearing me, the first sign of a building with life for a long time. The other buildings are empty, but I don't doubt that they hold several skeletons within their walls. There's two guys standing out beneath the light; I don't believe they're loitering, I know their game. The sex trade isn't one that takes a day off. I roll up with my window down and see two fairly thin dudes, both a couple of limber cats with ashes spreading from their lips. I flash a roll of cash to them and tell them to get in. They know what I'm here for; they know we're going back to my place so I can shoot my confessions into them. So I can pray to Nila through the act of fuckin', because that's what you do when you want to talk to her. You don't know that you're talking to her, though; you're not codependent of her. You are in control; she is merely giving her blessing as you dump your load into the person you're fuckin'. Acacia is too sexually repressed to understand what it is really like to screw your partner. Most are merely tickling tits and increasing the population; there's no real enjoyment of it anymore. But you can trace that all throughout our history. We have never been a people of sex, only a people of demonizing the orgasm in hopes to keep our women chaste and our men clean of fuckin' diseases. Condoms are not a thing that people should have, but we need them and they don't see that.

I ask for them both. I imagine they're twins because they look alike. Nothing special to them. Gray fuckin' fur getting drenched from the rain. Pure gray and green eyes, but no other distinguishing marks. They must have gotten away with so much when they were kids, no grown person would be able to differentiate between them. Simply identical. They're not from here; these cats were imported, probably through trafficking. I'm sure they're from the southern region of the world. Some place beyond the Acacian border. I can hear it in their accents as they're discussing my offer. I want them both; I don't want the general fuck. I want the fun; I'm going to get my fun. It's simply the way it is.

Their words are broken. They are southern, it's sad too. They were probably forced here after believing they were going to get a better life, but that's not my concern tonight. I'm a man of needs, a man of sickness. And my sickness needs release. They get in the car and I drive off. I'm not saying a damn thing; it's just one of them chatting to the air. My brain is holding a few words but it's all shit I've heard before. He's designating when they're getting their money and how far things can go. They fuck. They don't allow anyone to harm them. Leave the weird kinks out of it, anything involving feces and they're out of there. When the terms are out there, I give a slight grunt as agreement in hopes there is nothing more to say. My home is only a few more minutes away, though in the rain it feels as if we're driving across our country; as if the forgotten land has no end to it until we start to remember who we are as people. There aren't many that can, not many to make it out of there. Though there isn't anything supernatural, there is something about the presence of that area.

In a way we're energy, we can be transferred. It's why we teach ourselves to forget; why we're trained not to remember the souls we carry. I'd wonder who Nick is right now, but his spirit is still around. My delusions are

still around. I hope the goddess will drive them away—
drive them out from the walls of my home and into the
shattering open air. I'll be able to escape the dingy bottom
and smell the fresh scent of nature once again. She has
been gone for too long, how I miss her, but I have
forgotten her. We have all forgotten her.

The two boys wander into my home, lights flooding
the doorway as we remove our dampened clothing. I can
call them boys because they're young enough. Old enough
to meet the standards of our laws, yet young enough to
not understand what being a whore really means. They
don't know what'll happen to their bodies over the course
of the next few years; that some men are truly disgusting
in what they want. By their mid-twenties, I'm sure they'll
be ragged, but that is not something I feel necessary to
discuss, otherwise my thoughts would be debating the
entire night. I strip nude and lead them into the bedroom,
they are offered nothing from my home aside from a dry
night. They fall gracefully onto my mattress, two naked
bodies embedding themselves onto the thick white
comforter. I only watch them as they start kissing each
other. Their tongues intertwining furiously as their hands
massage each other. Though they are young, they are not
virgins. They understand the basic sense of arousal, or at
least understand my sense of arousal. Some things you
simply need to read into people. Sex is simply one of those
things.

Their moans are soft, deceiving, they want me to
believe that they are naïve, and though I can pretend, I am
not interested in fantasies. I want them for who they are.
The door closes slowly behind me, and my hand adjusts
my package as I move close to them. Although they are
like twins, I do notice the slight difference between them.

Darkness covers up the technicalities, light brings them forward. The silent one carries a small white tear drop beneath his eye. Though typical, it makes for a decent difference. When they are finished with their bit of foreplay, I cup my hand underneath the silent cat's chin and have him look at me. "Tonight, you're Frank." Looking sternly at the other one I sputter out, "And you're Allen."

There's no meaning to these names. It simply saves time; we're not in the dating business.

"Frank, I'd like for you to present your ass for me." He only nods at the request as his body moves into a more feral position. My hand brushes between his legs, fingers feeling around his tight little balls and softened cock. He lets out a slight moan as I do so. Cute. I smack his ass with my other hand; his moan gets slightly louder. I continue to smack, switching between cheeks, each slap getting harder. The room bursts into echoes between his boyish moans and the slaps bouncing from his ass. Still groping him, I can feel his cock get a little harder.

"Allen, eat him out for a little bit," I direct.

The talkative bitch is slightly taken aback by the command, but does not protest. He draws Frank's ripened hole to his face and buries himself between his cheeks. I can feel myself growing harder from watching them, their cries teasing my ears as one pleasures the other. I walk around them, cock standing at full attention. It has been neglected for years, but goddamn, has it been begging for this. Without warning, Frank shoves my throbbing meat into his mouth and starts swishing his tongue along it. Unprepared, I grip at the nightstand and let out a slight gasp before recollecting myself. I can't imagine the load that is going to be blasted, but I know I want it to last a long time.

I place a hand behind Frank's head and shove him down the full length of my member. I can hear him gurgle slightly, but he is a champ at it, he remains down and works hard along my shaft. I ain't no big thing, but I am proud to say I'm average. Most guys out there can't even say that. Allen can't even say that, I can see his from his current duties. But I am not here to judge them.

Allen's hand slowly lowers to his crotch, fingers tease himself as his penis grows to its full length. Slowly he plays with himself. I see him slide his tongue across Frank's hole before diving in again; Frank now gripping at my erection and sucking it off harshly. His head bobs jaggedly along my shaft. Though they were well-rehearsed, I get the feeling this one is still learning the trade. In a way, we all need to learn. There is no single individual out there who can be amazing all the time at sex. It's simply impossible.

I'm trying to imagine my prayers right now, but I can't. There are no words that can be spoken to send up to my goddess. I only have actions; I only have the entangling of our bodies waiting for the storm to calm down. But she is unpredictable. Gods are fickle that way; they're not easily read. They praise you for your loyalty and test you at the same time. Give you gifts and squeeze your balls because they know they've got you. They know you want to make them happy. It's why we all make stupid decisions; sacrificial monuments to our supreme ruler in the sky because he is angry. He is not satisfied with our worship and our tilling the fields with his name. He is not happy with the idols resurrected or the wars waged for him. He is only happy with our suffering. All living is suffering, which is why there is nothing when we pass. True nothingness is the bliss we all need to search for. But Acacians are afraid of nothing. They can't handle that there is nothing beyond living, that it takes years of peace within ourselves to attain this. Which is why heaven and hell are created. Diddle with kids; rob a grandma; and you're going to hell and drinking perverted semen for the rest of your adult afterlife. But if you're just; you swing on clouds and sing church music all day, like the fuckin' Mormons.

I yank myself out of this kid, slide the rubber on, and push him onto his back. Legs wide fuckin' open, I take no time in shoving my beast into him. Allen watches for a few moments before he dives into the kid's crotch. They slowly move into a sixty-nine while I pound the fuck out of Frank. I can hear his moans growing bolder as I slam myself into his body, grunts escaping me hard and quick. I am like a fuckin' ape makin' weird noises with my mouth. But that's what you do when you're screwing some people, make weird faces and noises; leave droplets of yourself inside them, and I fully intend on making them take a bit of me out the door.

Sweet sister of mercy, this dude is fuckin' tight. I can feel myself about to blow a fuckin' load, but it ain't the last of them. I got several bullets rousing in the gun, and this is only one of them. The haunting hour is almost on us. My eyes are crawling around the room as I shoot myself into this guy. It's a real skill to keep them from rolling back into my skull in moments of ecstasy. I could hear the disgruntled portions of my life leave my body as I grew weak from orgasm.

No signs of our spiritual friend. Smiling, a wave of relief crashes into me as I collapse onto the mattress. The haunting is not going to be appearing tonight; I suppose they're in the middle of rescheduling, but my prayers seemed to have worked. Sex is a form of prayer, a way to become one with the cosmos we are unable to see. Through orgasm, we can feel them roaming about invisibly. I can't say how many times I have had the unfortunate experience of crashing into them at the wrong moment. Little specks of space policing us with karma, how little we truly see of this world.

They're looking at me. I can tell they're wondering if they can leave now, but I am not a man that gets shortchanged. We're finishing up our night. I pull Allen closer to me and begin my work on him. The moon finally appears over the light rain as I explore this slut's body, fingers trudging through fur to find the sweet spots of my personal companion. He knows his work isn't over yet; he plays with me a bit more to earn the cash lying on the table. I can see him looking at it, reminding himself that it's why they're here. It's why they got in the car with me; it's why they entered my home. They will endure whatever to ensure they get that nice fat wad at the door.

His eyes avert back to me as I continue to massage his body; violent moans escape his teeth—jagged syllables thrown like knives into my ears. He truly played into his character—he deserved the pay. His companion lies there on the mattress; he wanted to do nothing more. His body was draped over the edge, eyes closed as if he were shutting us out; as if he did not want to hear what I was doing to his family. He doesn't like survival, but survival is an ugly whore. It takes a strong stomach to look her in the face.

I slowly move away from Allen. Pointing to the floor, he slides from the bed and grabs my cock, covered in my seed. "Clean it," I tell him, while grabbing a cigarette, dick still fuckin' hard from emptying myself into Frank. Allen slides his tongue from the base of my shaft to the tip. I shudder as I light my cig. The boy knows all the right twists. I regret that I have neglected any sexual endeavors for so long. Before these two entered my home, the desire had simply dissolved.

I tap Frank on the arm and motion for him to move closer. Smoothed out sheets become ruffled as he sits on my lap, legs spread open. I start jacking him off with one hand while the other ruffles his lips.

"I want you to cum on his face," I say as I stroke him faster.

Allen is working hard to get the cum off my cock. Frank says nothing, only whines a little as he opens his mouth allowing my fingers to invade. I can feel his hands grip at the bed; he's got the grip of a pregnant woman, springs straining between his fingers as I feel him get close. He doesn't take long to blow a load. I can feel his body growing furious as his dick comes close. Breaths become heavy, grips tighter, this bitch whines loudly as his seed bursts all over Allen's face. Frank collapses into me as his last drop shoots onto the little cocksucker.

Smirking, I put Frank to the side, let him rest. I think he's had his moment with god; there's a bit of enlightenment in his eyes. That is the beauty of the orgasm, they bring you closer to enlightenment than anything else in this world. They open the channels of your brain that are typically closed off on a regular basis. It's why sex is so important. Sure, there's procreation, but the real meaning is to continue to expand ourselves. Expand our own brain power since we don't use much of it anyway.

I tap Allen off my cock and bend him over the bed. A small gasp escapes him as he's thrown onto the sheets. I wrap it up again and force my way into his tight little ass, and does he have a tight little ass, goddamn! He's tighter than his friend here. My hips thrust firmly into his body; he starts to moan in hunger as he feels me fuck him like a slut. It's at this point I can't tell if he's really enjoying it or if he's acting. But that's their job, right?

Most of these dudes don't like the act of sex, but know how to use their bodies to get the cash. So they pretend to enjoy it and get a little thing for living expenses. No fuckin' harm, right? Most of us customers don't even care for the opinion of the person serving us. We use them, break them as far as we can, and fail to put them back together. They're there for us, meant for our abuse, for our spit, and they know this. It's understood; a silent agreement of sorts, not just lingering in the world of prostitution, but all customer friendly jobs. It's simply the way we are: demanding, immediate, angry.

The desolation between customer and whore is much more apparent. There is no sense of people between the two, only carnal vibrations leave our bodies when we meet. That is all this is, there is no love between me and these two boys, there is only escape. There is only release. There is only prayer.

There is rustling in my kitchen. I can feel the slender bodies of the twinks I picked up cuddled against me. Soft purrs emit from their heavy sighs as they sleep comfortably, unaware of the intruder lingering about my home. In a way, it's a blessing they're not awake. Handling some threat with two unpredictable persons is something I'd rather not bother with. I inch off my bed, ensuring their uninterrupted slumber as I stalk through the hallway and into the kitchen. I hear the cabinets closing, pots rustling, as if some asshole is going to make dinner at my place. The worst kind of thief, a fucker who eats the food I pay not to eat. That's what we do in this country; pile groceries and food on our plates only to shuffle the last half-eaten morsel into the garbage. And who benefits from it? I suppose the homeless, but they are no more dogs than the rest of us. We're all civilized beasts here, but there is no reason anyone should act like it I suppose. I've no real protection, there's no gun anywhere in my home. I'm told that you need a gun. I'm told that the best protection is to fire off bullets at any person who feels like intruding. It's okay to kill in the name of standing your own ground, protecting yourself. Acacia is a gun driven world. Most living here would rather die than allow anyone to take their weapons away from them. It's a competition here. Do you love God more or the gun more?

Fuck the gun nuts! Their propaganda won't persuade me to buy one. I won't carry bullets in my home. I won't feed them stories of success against unwanted company. Those assholes are not even people, they're third rate; the type of assholes we should treat as we do the homeless on the street. Get a goddamn job, well I can assure you, those National Gun Association fucks have little jobs aside from ensuring access to the heaviest weaponry a wife beater can buy. Who is safe from who? This is exactly what they are afraid of. The exact argument they make. What do you do without protection? How can you stop the invasion?

There's a flip-flop on the floor. If the little lab mouse were here, he'd bitch at me for having a goddamn shoe in the middle of the house. I suppose the same could be said about the ghost lingering in my past. Emptiness is a state of mind, but so is being full. The state of being empty isn't always as depressing as one would make it out to be. I've filled myself over the past couple years and it has brought me here, back to emptiness. But I suppose I need to watch it as too much of this state of mind leads to the vultures dissecting your body. It's amazing they're still feral creatures; that they never evolved like the rest of Acacia. Bodies meandering about, waiting for the fresh meat to drop dead on the roadside. Some people are best served fresh, but I don't know nothing about that. It's not civilized.

I pick up this fuckin' shoe and raise it as I wander into my own kitchen. What the fuck was I to do, huh? Fuck, I wish I had heels, at least then I could stab a guy, but I ain't no crossdresser. Though I've seen plenty out there I'd like to fuck. I'm inching farther into the room and flip on the lights. Saying nothing, I see nothing. It's empty. But I know I heard something. I know I heard something messing with my stuff. I slowly turn around to ensure I'm seeing the full picture here, but it's all as I left it. There was no one here, and yet, I heard someone.

How far is my mind falling? How far is the abyss dragging me? I still can't feel the air beneath me as my body free falls into her. Nila! Did I not pray to you to help me end this crisis? Did I not send you two seeds of sacrifice so that I may finally know what it is to rest? What madness enters my home now? What more must I encounter so that I may finally know peace? I lower the shoe to my side in hopes that I may find these answers, but they were never here. The twinks only filled me with a momentary lapse of reason; something that we all need to experience once in a while. I have a feeling I'll be seeing them more often, reason is something I need to lose; I wonder if it will help me understand the nothingness that awaits us in the end.

In the beginning, there was nothing. In the end, there will be nothing waiting for us. This is not a state of misunderstanding, or a moment of depression. This is not atheism at its best. This is the truth. There will be nothing there when we leave this planet. But it takes time to find it; time to find the exact state of being. It takes time to know oneself. I have not fully understood my own soul, it's why I'm waving a shoe in my kitchen, because I have not yet found the emergency ticking beneath my heart. I have only found tragedy, and she is not the company I seek.

My ears twitch. The rustling has begun again. I hear something in my office, papers rummaging around. I take the shoe with me, false hope of something being there. As

I enter, I see him. Sandal dropping to the ground, I only utter his name. "Nick... ." The last letter trails off into the madness of this night. The blinds are open; a half moon shines through giving a glimmer of his body. Auburn fur tints my eyes as I try to believe what I am seeing.

He doesn't say anything. He only stares out the window. There's something cold about him, something about the nature of his visit. I can't find the strength to utter what I want, little gasps and weird noises escape my muzzle as I stand in awe. My feet trudge forth across the carpet as I reach out. I have to know if he has really shown himself. I have to feel him one last time. I never got to feel the one I loved for a final moment—only ashes and charred fur. I'm only left with a memory of what his touch was like, and the memories fade off into the distance. He was just like any other person. He came and went. He broke too easily

"Where did your mind go to when they wheeled my charred body out from the house?"

He is taking me back. It's as if I can see the flames. Like I was still there. The old house collapsing beneath the fire; men wheeling him out; but I am not there. I am only seeing what the phantom wants me to see. I am inside tragedy. A spectator watching memories of myself point out the body of my own loved one. I can feel my own tears spread from my eyes. Why does this spirit collapse my consciousness, why does it push me into this tremor of time?

"I was nowhere," I respond. I can never account for my mental being, I can only account for my physical state. Where my mind wanders off to, I'll never really know. Maybe that's a good thing.

Flakes of fur begin to snow in the room. His body grows black before me, the moonlight saving no detail from me. How I wish I knew how to love; how I wish I knew how to love him. I fear I never understood this; more of that fear grows into reality over time. I will never truly understand this demon that lingers about, but he is here now. How I wish I could love him, much like how I wish I could love Ely. But they are far from me now; they have crossed over to different paths and I am not to see them again. I am to stare at the nothingness that awaits me at the end, the real enlightenment. Suffering is living, the rest is just a novel bled out from my fingers.

"You are the shepherd that refuses to let his flock roam, and still you are unhappy." His voice cringes in the darkness as he disappears.

What confrontation has left me? Beauty, without its forms, is still beauty. Are we all on the same path to madness, or is there a light between the emptiness I fail to see?

The morning will come soon. The boys will be awake. I waddle back into the bedroom and lie between them to enter the state of being whole again. To run from the flock that haunts my home. In my own body, I feel that I have let them go, but they cling to me. If I cling to them, then how long until I follow into the afterlife? How long until I leave into the abyss? I'm already partially there. Mother of all things, what is in this world to save me from myself?

There's someone outside of my home. I am breathing to keep myself calm, but I fear breaking down soon. It's meditative and my heart is soft. I know it is only myself out there. My guilt peering through my home.

It was there the night we had to put the fox in the ground—beast-like shadow simply lingering around whenever the big shit hits the fan. I didn't want to see it then, but guilt is no hallucination. I have dreamed scarier visions than shadows in the moonlight. I'm starting to wonder if I am really awake or if this is another dream. It wouldn't be so uncommon anymore. My own consciousness is a wavering state, not set to remain whole for a moment. Guilt is still out there, staring at me, I can't see his eyes, but I know he sees me staring back at him, I believe he means to kill me, yet I mean to kill him. There is no savior to keep us from taking each other from this world, no one to stop us; we're merely beasts in this moment. My heart is slowing down now; I can hear the quiet of the outside perfectly. He is now moving, dark figure moving towards the window, I start to breathe faster. He remains faceless, he remains unidentified, I grab a cig from the drawer in this room, keeping quiet, the boys are still sleeping, such angels, we're all angels when we sleep. Three one two, three one two, three one two, three one two, three one two, three one two three one two, three one two three, I meditate. His footsteps are leaving their mark on the grass, he's finally stopped at the window, yet he is faceless, a simple vision, unknown man, demons coming to haunt me in my vulnerable moments. I feel alone now and they know it, they can bubble up whenever they please because I have no protection from them. I will sleep until morning. I will not let them take me. It is not my time yet....

Lorenzo was an asshole pimp. A maggot with a large imprint on the world, and for years I tried to stay out of his way. The first time I met him, I had this sickness at the bottom of my stomach. His presence disrupted my bowels to the point where they wanted to escape, but composure is one of the few things I have. He was a sickness that I wish I had cured years ago. Pacifism was never the way to really solve his existence; prison was never really the correct route for him. We are time; time lost to searching. Time gained in finding answers, but at the cost of sacrifice and I have given all too much to the father of the cosmos for me to sit patiently. Karma is not the woman in control of the situation anymore.

We met at a dingy club after a recommendation from The Doctor, an old friend who performed backwards surgeries for discounted prices because the private nature of health care was failing us all. The Doctor specialized in everything; it's why I loved him. Though it has been years since we have chatted, I still wonder what he is doing today. I suppose he found his own circus. There are simply too many that linger with illness.

This piss-poor excuse for a club was the back alley of music. Hardcore metal bands that sounded like pipes were being shoved through their asses blared through dark red and graffiti-plastered walls as I moved through the crowd of vampire-lookin' folks. It wasn't the best sight to say the least, but it didn't matter. I was there on some business. At the time I wasn't in love and I needed a little release. It's never a bad idea to have a good fuck, and to help someone financially just makes the deal sweeter. Though then I was naive to the nature of the sex industry as a whole. I never knew of the pimps beating their bitches into submission; the drugs pumped through dozens of individuals so they will never leave. Sex trafficking is ignored by the rest of the world because sex is gross. We're not grown up yet, we're aware and we're keeping it silent because why the fuck should we help the unmentionables? It's a whole new class warfare and no one gives a fuck. That was me, and I still buy into the fun, though most of the ones that swing by are on their own. They haven't been chained behind closets by the stronger alphas yet, though I often wonder how long it takes for it to happen.

I make my fuckin' way and I see the bastard, smokin' cigs at a table with a full pitcher of beer. If you're going to kill yourself, you have to do it in style. He had balls you wouldn't want to fuck with. They say wolves are bad people; that they're people who thrive on controlling the illness that surrounds all of us. I've never been too sure how true that was, but I know it is true of that man. You could see it in his eyes, he was hungry, but not for one thing or the other. He wanted to be in control and he was with this line of people he owned. That's right, owned. They were simply toys in his business and that's how the customers treated them. It's how I treated them, like a transaction for a good time. I could blab about how ashamed of myself I am, but what's the fuckin' point? It doesn't change the situation, and it never will. Being forgiven for your sins only works when you want to be holy, I simply want to understand the purity of emptiness which I have yet to find.

Morals are the blockade to finding out the true nature of yourself. The nature of who you are, who you are going to be, and who you were. Though I'm sure everyone finds this through their own sense of prayer and meditation, I find the peace sitting along the linings of my flesh when I'm in the middle of fuckin' someone. Sex is the key to finding the holy lands, the grail that escapes us. Sex is nirvana in little bursts; that moment of truly being, and it's fuckin' beautiful.

Pimps are not illegal; the act of prostitution is not illegal, though the act of selling another individual as a slave is. There are moments where you tend to believe that your government has some sense of intelligence among them, then you hear the severity of their control and wonder if things are truly ideal like you had voted for. Acacia is a country founded on freedoms, and as the years have trudged through, it feels we continuously regress into the very monsters we fought against when we established ourselves as a country in this world. Red-blooded Acacians scream about the faggots ruining their countries, of the countless fetuses littering dumpsters in the back alleys, of the children being forced to exercise because they actually believe exercising is a danger to their health. Real common fuckin' sense drenched out of the common man through the brainwashing of daytime television. Go back to sleep, it is not time to wake up yet, but I'm already fuckin' awake, man. I'm awake and I fuckin' see what you're doing.

President. Child molester. Keep us warm and stupid; keep us fed off fast food grease and heart-consuming preservatives because we are not controlled enough. We are not in your jumpsuits yet, we are only listening to your words through our newscasters. Freedom of speech through the corporations selling our fuckin' views and replacing our own way of thinking with funny home videos of kids demolishing themselves in sports and drunk adults pissing themselves at family gatherings. We're fuckin' cute like that. We're fuckin' cute enough to ignore the real disease that is consuming us. But what the fuck do I know, right? I'm just some fuckin' dude smokin' a cig while we allow the democratic republic to pump our veins with painkillers and caffeine. We're not dead yet, but we will be soon. They'll want our bodies when we're dead. They can use them. Research. Chemical research on all things war. All things murder. All things mass-market.

I was fuckin' glad for prostitution being legal that night I met Lorenzo. First goddamn time seein' the bastard, so I walk up to this asshole in the club, all nervous and shit as he looks me over. I didn't say much aside from what I was lookin' for and flashed some cash at him which seemed to make him more interested in my presence. I didn't give a fuck what he thought of me, I just wanted to fuck for little bit. I never knew how much of a disgusting being he was until I got to know him a bit more. Wrapped underneath his arm was my future boyfriend at the time, Nick, slim-fit fox resting his head against the wolf's chest. Typical couple, everything all good in the bed of roses, but thorns mask themselves. It wasn't my concern at the time.

He counted the cash and was happy with it. I expected the dude to point me through a door so I could get a room, but no. Nick gets up from this guy's arm and leads me away. I'm thinkin' he's going to take me to some good merch, but realize later that he was the merch. He led me to this backroom in the place; flickering lights exposed a worn cot and pukish-green walls. Although he displayed himself for me, I could see the slight glimpse of shame in his face. He didn't want to be there, but he was there for whatever reason. He was there and I was going to find my own nirvana. I never knew what it was like to fuck someone while they cried. Beneath my roaring groans, I heard his whimpers. The fur of my hands had grown matted with his tears. Although I had paid for him, I could never shake the feeling that I had raped him. I was his rapist and later became his lover. In Acacia, there are laws against rape, but we are not a culture of believing the victim. In most cases, the victim is shamed and disowned by the society. Would they have put Nick through the same if he came out about that night? These were only some of the questions that ran through me afterwards. I was gentle with him; my sense did not fail. There was no light that lead me to the world of enlightenment. This quick lapse in time was merely lost on me. It was my moment of martyrdom, killing my method of clearing my own mind for the sake of keeping the fox's sanity.

When I finished, I whispered an apology in his ear and took my leave. I eventually became a regular with Lorenzo, but he always disgusted me. He always left me sick. I never knew what he did to his victims. I never saw the imprints he left on them. But I have always known the scars held by the poor lost fox now wandering the universe. Lorenzo is not a man that understands what it is to exist, he only understands what it is to drain the lives around him. He is hungry, and he has always been hungry. Lorenzo has always been the living devil; his victims have never heard the voices of angels. But that is simply how it goes in this realm of existence. This thing we ignore. We do not know how to handle the suffering of others, but we endure like it is our fault. We're sorry individuals offering prayers to cure the virus. We fail at realizing the need to act. I fail at realizing the need to act. I am no more at fault than the rest of our friends, but what does that mean to any of us now?

We thrive on half-moons. We thrive on shit that's half-full, half-empty because we need something to reach for in our lives. Otherwise we wander around the shithole apartment aimlessly wondering what to do next because it's all fuckin' bullshit and meaningless. But he wasn't meaningless, he kept me from the abyss some days, though while dead he leads me further. Ely wasn't meaningless, but what did we want to know about each other aside from that I was a guy with cash and he needed a paycheck? Usual customer experiences, five fuckin' star ratings for the company.

I'm sitting in this restaurant. This place is empty. I've always wondered how they stay open with no customers and piss-poor excuses for cultural food. The waitress brings my meal, television blaring dumbass talk show hosts believing they know what's politically right for Acacia, but she don't know shit. Her guests don't know shit. They're not enlightened. They're not awake. She sets my food down, syrup drizzled over fried chicken with some fucked up excuse for fried rice. Scientists often wonder if chicken will ever evolve like we did, but they're behind in the scene. Feral beasts getting sliced up and fed to the rest of us, but it's no different if they sliced me up and fed me to the colonies inside our cities. Some folks like eating the intelligent few of the world, and that's fine if there's consent and no one knows about it.

I don't ask questions anymore. Some folks are just not desirable to me. There's some justice in that, though I am unsure where it is. I dig my fork into the meat, tongue lapping at the syrup dripping down, sweet spice attacking the taste buds. It isn't bliss, though how am I to feel any enjoyment when I am lost? She has simply given me sustenance and I have paid her for it. We all pay for our own survival, though it feels as if we are treating ourselves. And maybe some of us are when eating at hole-in-the-wall restaurants; maybe I felt this would be a treat, but shouldn't I have known better? I suppose at some point we learn of our mistakes and grow from them, but I am merely existing. How much room is there to grow when you are a body pandering about, when your moon has grown empty and you're on the last bit of life? Though on the other hand, it's amazing how hard that last little bit of life fights to live

I'm eating and I'm watching this fuck up tell us how she thinks the transgendered community shouldn't be treated like people. How entitled they are to change their gender identities to what they want. But it's not about want. She misses the entire fuckin' point. It was never about the desire for another gender; it's about the need. It's about being born the wrong way and correcting the mistake to be who you truly are. Sadly, she cannot hear me through electric currents and shitty speakers. She is simply misinformed and prejudiced, and that's not shocking at all. Acacia is built on hate in a way. We killed the original citizens of this land, took their women, beat their children, and killed their men so we could become our own community. We are a country of violence; we are a country of hate filled with hardened souls of love. But love isn't winning here; she is merely surviving like I am. Last bit of life left in us, last bit of fight in our fists because fuck! We're at the goddamn corner, broken teeth on the ground but we can't give the fuck up yet. We can't fuckin' die yet. We need to fix something, we need to fill that goddamn half-moon that hangs above our windows at night. We are tired of her promises to one day grow full. We are tired of hearing she will be strong for our woes. We are tired of hearing the bullets stream down from her mouth. We are tired of the war.

Somewhere out there, there's a bomb going off, and that's okay in most of our minds because we're ignorant folk. Don't show us the violence. It'll taint our sunglasses and sunshine worldview. We have not yet thrown ourselves to anarchy; we are only evolving to the point of smelling the stench of napalm in the morning and saying, "Whelp, it happened again, what can you do?" And we do that with everything. Kids shooting kids in the schools; adults shooting adults in the grocery store. God wanted rifles, God hates the Muslims. Kill them all, fuck them all, leave no opponent untouched by his fists. Leave all Christians alive, you can trickle out the wrong ones later. And still they wonder why people fight against scriptures. God is not in my heart. He cannot heal me. He cannot heal my scars. God is only mascara; he'll rub off one day and my bullet holes will be revealed when that happens.

I asked Nick to kill me once. It was shortly after our first time together. I gave him the fuckin' gun because I couldn't live with the first time we had sex. I always saw the tear-soaked mattress and I couldn't bear to think of it. We were in a hotel room at the time, ceiling stained with tobacco ash, walls covered in piss-yellow. He started to undo my pants as I inhaled the sweetness, but I stop him. I left a gun on the bed and ask him to end me because of my indiscretions. But he could not. His fingers were not strong enough to pull the weak trigger. We hadn't been fuckin' for long, but he broke down. Dropped the gun and told me that he wasn't supposed to be there. He wasn't supposed to be blowing guys for cash. The fox told me he was supposed to be three states away but met the monster on the internet. He was roped into this life with the promise of something better. And that's how it always goes, son. That's how it always goes. They get you, offer you sacrifices of gold and honey, but you only get raped of your own fuckin' soul. And what choice do you have when you get there?

I have a problem. I grow addicted to people too easily. In the span of that single moment, I latched myself onto him. Nick was my everything from then on out. My full fuckin' moon, man, and it was fuckin' beautiful when we escaped it all. I left that world behind with him in hand. We moved cities, took on new names and identities. We thought we were free. In the end, it didn't matter. When you're runnin' from fire, it eventually catches up to you. It catches up and you slowly turn into ash. We're cemeteries in a way, carrying memories of our dead until we venture off into the afterlife.

I never had enough time to settle with Ely. He saw through the windows of my bones, read the sickness lingering inside me. He knew I was getting too far attached to him, maybe it was better he escaped the poison ivy growing from my fingertips. It wouldn't have been long before the vines wrapped themselves around him, but that's the nature of anyone's addiction. It all starts slow.

You take a sip of coffee, tell yourselves that's it, that you won't do it much. Next thing you fuckin' know, you're downin' Monsters and energy drinks every five hours because caffeine is a hell of a drug. People are a hell of a drug. Their warmth is a hell of a drug, y'all. Some days you just need a warm body to keep the voices away in the morning.

The door rings as he enters. Southern fall heat glistens his shadow as his footsteps mark the piss-green tile. Afternoon glare drizzling over the man's fur, bits of gray lingering about the air, it took me a moment to adjust my eyes to him. The devil had walked in. It's not often you encounter the hand responsible for your own suffering, but in certain stages of consciousness, I suppose anything is possible. Only he isn't a figment. His body is pure. The devil Lorenzo has finally made his appearance, though I did not search for him. I only pray to the spirits he does not see me, but prayers are only a glimmer of unanswered hope.

This motherfucker sees me lapping up what little there is of my meal, and grins. Big fuckin' ass-eatin' grin. You could see the fuckin' shit on his teeth, his smile was so fuckin' wide. Dumbass come walkin' up to me like I give a damn about his fuckin' presence. I'm just tryin' to eat my fuckin' food, man. I'm not looking for company at the moment. But alas, peace was sure to end soon. We're not creatures of peace. We're monsters of war. Always have been. We knew about killing each other way before we grew civilized, before we evolved into the children we are today. We ain't grown yet, but we understand a bullet to the chest means some motherfucker is dead. Killing is so easy for folks, man. It's simply who we are. I feel like chokin' this lil' bitch ass that's sitting down across from me. He pulls out a cig and just says, "It's been a long time, man. I see you're still alive."

All I can fuckin' say, syrup on my motherfuckin' lips is, "Shit, it happens. Other folks survive, I might as well be in line with them." I wipe the shit off my lips with a napkin, drain the beast out of me, and pretend I'm grown for a fuckin' minute.

He inhales a large amount of smoke as the waitress brings him a menu. He's not interested in the food yet. Nods for her to go away until he's ready. That's the kind of dick this bitch is, man. Just knows how to communicate with a look or a gesture. He knows how to get his respect even though he's the monster. "You miss me? Miss seein' this mug around? Where you been gettin' your tail at, man?"

Smug fuck. "I miss a lot of things. A piece of ass was merely an angel I could count on in life. Such a luxury is no longer around, I'm afraid. I got around." I pull out a pack of smokes and light up—sweet nectar lingering on my tongue, cooling the anxiety bubbling in my fingers. I stopped taking Vicodin the moment this juice hit my tongue. Fuck the ash, the mere taste of smoke was all I needed and I was good again. We stare at each other for a moment. He could see the hell inside of me, spiraling in my chest. He could see the urges to kill him subside with a puff.

It was as if he had forgotten the whole thing. He wanted business as usual again, but I am no longer a customer in his shop. The bar closed down, man, and folks moved on. I shredded my rewards card with him and found better ass, and it was good. It was like when God said "Let there be light," if he ever existed.

"You leave any other troubles behind you?" I ask him. You always want to know the story of your enemy. Even if you plan on doing nothing with the information, you simply want the story. Why we are so drawn to the struggles of other individuals is something I will never understand. But we are. We are so addicted to the soap operas of our lives that we have to stop ourselves just to hear the story. We're all sad individuals inside. We're all lost to the stars, soaking up the drama because we got nothin' else.

"I've only been out for a day, and you already diggin' shit the fuck up, man. Mind your own shit."

Defensive. We're all defensive, yet we fail to hide ourselves. I stare him down. Nothin' more to say, just grabbing his fur for my archive files.

"You haven't aged well, Lorenzo. You still got the game? Been out of practice for a while." Maybe that was taking it a bit too far, but I've nothing else to lose anymore. He took back what was his years ago. There's no stakes here; only two men with bitterness in their bones.

"Fuck off, man. You got no right comin' at me like that. You stole my merch man, it was just business." He's apologetic, yet there is barely a drop of sincerity in him.

"I still see him some days." He stays silent. "Is there a reason you've decided to sit here and not anywhere else?" I ask directly. There really isn't a need for him to be here. He's not making amends and I'm not accepting apologies. We're simply two souls sitting across from one another with pointless dialogue.

"I can't even remember what he looked like. His face is empty every time I think of him. I could probably put something there if I wanted to, but the boy is lost in my mind somewhere and I don't feel the need to dig him up anymore. You're haunted though, poisoned by the death of someone you fucked. Could anyone every truly love a whore? Knowing what they've done to themselves, to their bodies, did you really believe you could love him?" His arms fold on the table, cig jetting from his lips now. He appears to be getting angrier with the thought. His eyes grow wild, as if he was seeing angels on the baseball field, madness in the family urn.

"What boundaries are there? Is it really as constricted as you make it out to be? Is it not formless, leading us down our own uncertain paths? I loved him. Ignorant as I was, I loved him. Though I sometimes wonder if that was my mistake, I would still give my soul to the train tracks to be able to feel his warmth again." I stir the straw in my soda, sulking at the confessions pouring from my tongue.

I hear the faint chuckle from his lips. He inhales again, smoke dancing about as it pours into my face. "We're ghosts in the glass; not meant to ever be whole. Dog, you carry burdens that should have been let go, yet your grip is tighter than the dead tugging on the chain of your life. You are without sin aside from love. She is poison. She is time. She is not your mistress any more. You are absolved." He said nothing else as he got up and left. I watched him become a shadow in the sun. I watched him dissolve from me; even the living come and go. My presence is simply an open house, waiting for folks to buy her, yet I am not quite at prime market value. Investments are not a wise choice at the moment, though some day I might be worth something, and those folks may feel regret for their choice. Until then, I'll listen to the dead talk to me. Their whispers have yet to kill me.

He left a card on my table. Business as usual. Address. Number. Price. He doesn't miss a beat, the fuck. I paid the lady at the restaurant. Shitty place, but I keep coming back. I am now outside of a house on the semi-bad part of town. When you in a bad business, man, you don't stick to the bad neighborhoods. You reside in places you can stand to see in the twilight, but are uneasy in the dark. I suppose you could call it middle class, but the margin is so far out there, it's hard to pinpoint what that means anymore. So I'm sitting in my car and I'm drinking the last of an energy drink, my brain can't function without them anymore. It tells me every morning to drink one or else it won't fuckin' work. Caffeine, another addiction, another day, another death. I'm chugging this fuckin' thing and I'm staring at the doors of the house. It's rare to see a home with double doors, only flashy folks want them. They're not practical. I know he's in there, waiting for me. He wouldn't have reached out to me if he didn't want me here. He's not the type of guy to just show up for nothing. He wants something. My cash. They always want the cash, man. We're all just walking cash signs, take a fuckin' buck from my pocket, and get some weird subscription service. Pay bills. Be an adult. Be a member of society. Don't fuck bitches because it's immoral and against God. Well, fuck your god and your fuckin' society, man. I'm just here to throw the cash on the table. Don't preach to me about sanity, man. You'll never understand it. You'll only understand business. They're not the same. They're never the fuckin' same.

The devil had houses all over Acacia. He was an operation—a cartel. He preferred them with double doors, though I can't imagine why. He has a house here. He has people that work for him here. They are his eyes when he is away. I suppose that's how he caught up to Nick and I. The network spotted us. They reported us, and he served his own bit of punishment. Lorenzo was always a hanging judge.

The doors look angry. Dark brown wood peering over me, and I ain't even reached 'em yet. I get out of the car; walk up the lead steps, the house hasn't been fixed in a long time. I knock, the thuds from my fists echoing behind the doors. Slowly, chains begin to unlock and disassemble in the background and the doors creak open. And there he stood, darkness surrounding him, eyes lightly glowing in the afternoon light.

"You know why I'm here," is all I say and he waves me in.

"You wanna see the new merch? I got a new batch in the room up ahead. We're still groomin' them, but I like to show off, especially to old customers." He stops midway and forces a grin. "Now listen, shit's in the past, stays in the past. If it wasn't you, it would have been some other mangy fuck to do me in, that's just the way it is. But don't go takin' shit that ain't yours. You're not a hard one to kill."

I simply nod with confidence. He seems to be all right with the gesture and begins to move again for the room. Most other folks wouldn't want me back. I rather expected him to shun me away, but this is capitalism. You don't give a damn about your customers. If one steals from you, you raise your guard and cut off the hand on the second try. "Once you take a look at the new ones, I'll show you what's available. I can't let you fuck the ones we're prepping. They need to be untouched until I'm ready to release them. It's an art. It takes time."

The door slowly sways back as we enter. Dim-lit room, nasty cots littered about, bodies shaking from being cold. They have IV drips in their arms, draining all sorts of poison into their bodies. He needs to make them submissive. He needs to make them his. I remain composed. I remain unreadable, though I am horrified. Some of the boys were barely living, ribs sticking out from lack of food, noses dripping with blood from being beaten over and over. Wounded souls, there is no savior for you; there is no savior for the dead.

We continue down until the last bed. Windows blacked out, no outside light allowed in. They must not know what life is like. They must not remember how the sun looks, or how the moon feels when it bathes your back. These bodies will never be allowed to understand what it is they have been lured into. Teens, I'm sure, young tight ones, some virgins maybe, all coerced into laying here and being raped of who they are. They will soon be without family, without identity. They will soon be without love. But that's all right, there's a select few out there who need to know what a good fuck is, and they get the money for it. Inside I weep for them, but I cannot allow my tears to reach the floor. I am an island, there is no amount of love I can have anymore. That is how I have to reside now. May these teens find peace someday.

It is strange that I am able to walk inside these walls, but who am I to Lorenzo aside from a stack of cash? I bleed money in his eyes. The past is absolved with the expectation of longstanding business.

I look at the last bed, teeth-white fur jutting around. He is not taking the meds well, it is a shame to think if he will survive. But he is not concerned with him. This is merchandise, not people, and merch can be tossed in the dumpster and forgotten. I stare a bit more at the body, the fur all too familiar to me. Although weak, the boy's scent lingers around my nostrils bringing back after-dark memories of ourselves together. Ely, lost to the wind, we have met again. Whether this life has brought us together or our passing is simply coincidence is something I'm not entirely concerned with. I can only tremble at the horrors he has been suffering, little lab mouse.

"You know how to pick 'em," I let out as I try to maintain composure.

"It's why we're the best at what we do. You want this one on preorder?" He chuckles as we both stare at his fragile arms cradling himself. I can see the needle digging deeper into his veins as he moves violently around the bed. His pain is silent, but visible. I say nothing. I want to touch him. I want to get him from the bed and to a hospital. He doesn't look like he can live much longer. Ely, I wonder if you know of the poison circling your blood. I doubt you do, yet he does not care for you. Ely, I have missed you. I have not thought up your body in my kitchen as I do with Nick, but I have missed you. I don't know if you have felt the same for me, but it shouldn't matter now. You are hurting. If I leave you, it will continue. Ely, I cannot say goodbye to you again.

Lorenzo walks back to the door. I follow, conjuring some method of escape, but I am not fast on my feet. I need to get him out. I need to do it now. I need to kill the wolf. My eyes grow dark, I cannot see much of what is in front of me, it is so loud in here. The boys moaning and twitching, cots creaking, bodies dancing, this house is not a quiet one. I like quiet homes. You can hear yourself think. You can hear yourself talk to the wind. Sometimes it's all right to ensure you talk beyond the faces in front of you. I feel dizzy as I walk behind him. The room is spinning slightly, rocking and spinning, growing darker, I can't explain the surroundings anymore. I don't feel faint, but I don't feel like I'm alive. I can't wait much longer. I can't wait much longer. I can't fuckin' wait much longer. Spinning…spinning…spinning… .

My hands grab his waist. I am slamming his head into the floorboards. His voice is muffled; I don't allow him to scream. He doesn't deserve to scream. He doesn't deserve the relief of being alive. Pain is not something he has felt. I can hear his breathing slowly fading, hands around neck, tongue jutting out, he is not going to live much longer. I don't know if they have heard me. I don't care if they have heard me. This my prayer to the goddess of death, may she take his soul elsewhere in the world, may his soul never injure another in this life. I feel his body grow limp. His arms slowly lose strength. His eyes lose signs of life. I feel every little moment as he dies in my hands. There's a difference between the dead and the sleeping. The sleeping are still heavy, they still make noise. The dead simply become paperweights of the earth. They are only meant to return to dust so the planet can flush, but I don't think he'll be growing any flowers when time passes. He has nothing left to offer the world. No name, no body, he is simply erased by my hands; the blood is singed to my palms. His blood is poison; his blood is crack waiting to pollute your body. Lorenzo, move on into whatever else this existence offers. I do not wish to see you in the next life. I crack his neck to ensure he cannot return, the boys still singing loudly. I hear footsteps approaching.

I slide off to the side, hide in the darkness, pray they cannot see me. An individual enters the room, runs toward the body. There's a hammer next to the dresser here, I grab it. I do not want to use it. Some trafficking circles use tools to beat the submissiveness into their merchandise. Lorenzo was someone who would abuse anyone. There've been several stories in the underground of how cruel he would be to some of the boys he recruits. He never harmed their faces, but I am sure that this hammer has broken some ribs.

The person says nothing. I don't see him, I only see his shadow. I turn the hammer to its back, nail remover out and lethal. I jump out of the dark corner and rush behind him, slamming the sharp edges into the back of his head. I continue to wail on him, bits of blood and fur flying in the atmosphere. He will not have much longer to live. He has not seen me. I smash him, and smash him until I can hear him breathe no more. No one else is coming. Not yet. Must move fast. Cannot waste time. Two dead men on my hands. I leave them there. They will not haunt me. I will not look for their spirits. I run up to Ely. Poor Ely. How you have suffered. I rip out his IV and run out the door. Still no one is coming. I fear there is another man here, but I dare not go searching for him. I toss the boy into the back seat, twilight approaching us now. I get in my car, keep looking down in case anyone can see me. I drive off, frantic at first, but eventually even out. I drive far away. Get on the freeway. Speed through lanes. Circle the whole city. I return home eventually. I return home and bring him into my bedroom. I lay him to sleep. I let his body fight the poison inside him. When he regains consciousness, we can talk. Sleep now, Ely. You're safe.

It's raining outside. It hasn't rained in a while. Maybe it has and I haven't been paying attention. Some days blend so close together it's hard to tell when a new one begins. It's all time, it's all cyclical, we're all moving along with it. I'm staring at the droplets slamming into the windows as he sleeps. Nature is angry today, the storm is strong. I'll be surprised if we keep power.

He's been asleep for a couple of days now. I suppose if I had a lot of dope in me, I wouldn't want to be awake either. I come in to check on him every so often, he still breathes, he screams sometimes. I think the nightmares are getting to him. But he is not the only one here.

Nick's ghost still haunts me here. My guilt has not dissolved from me. They are slowly venturing off. They know of the little lab mouse; they know he is here. Why wouldn't they? They're delusions I've created out of grief—how I have loved torturing myself! But Ely makes everything go quiet when he's around. I'm at peace with him, even during the storms, I'm at peace. Little lab mouse, don't leave me again. I don't know how far I will go next time. I don't know what my demons have in store. I fear they cannot be trusted, but how can I know?

No one's ever said they couldn't trust their conscious state of mind, they've only said they couldn't trust themselves. I am not myself. This is my body, but I am one in a few things inside me. How my heart still beats is beyond my comprehension.

Meditation only lasts for so long. I only have a select limit of willpower before it breaks and dives into the black hole of rage again. I am not safe, I have never been safe. I still feel the flames of the past coming for me. My feet have traveled far in my escape but he continues to catch up to me. I have killed the man responsible, but he cannot leave me alone. I can't say sorry anymore, I can't live with him anymore. Nick, how far must I go to keep you from haunting me? I am not the man who killed you, yet you remain with me. Nick, why must I love the torment you purge into my body? My hands have worked so hard for you, when can I be let go? I see you now, walking outside in the rain, and yet you are dead. You're at the grocery store, but you are dead! You touch me and still your hands are warm, but we have laid you to rest years ago. When will you finally be at peace, spirit?

I am waiting for an answer, but it will not come. I love you, but I cannot love you anymore in this life. We are not meant to be together here, I will meet you one day in the next life. Maybe then we can be safe together but not now! Never now! Ease my soul dear lover, ease it, and leave me be now. There's new fur in my bed, and I have been slowly growing around him like I did with you, spirit. I am slowly growing attached, and now I feel there is a chance for us two to live in this life together. An unattainable soul has given me a chance, I hope. Pathetic as I am, I dream of us being together someday. I dream of lying with him as a lover and not a customer. Yet dreaming is my illness, I can still grab onto him and pray to the spirits he can return my feelings. Feelings that I have buried since he left, since I got too attached to him and he left! Though he may leave again, I pray that he does not.

Spirit, I beg you, leave me now. Allow me the ability to create new art with this passion, let it remain formless yet able to gain form. Let us bind to each other, yet remain boundless. Such impossibilities are what I ask of this world and of the spirits watching us. Nick, lover of the past, rest your bones now, rest them and be happy.

"So you killed him?"

Some folks are good at hiding their expressions. Ely was a person I could rarely read. There was so much indifference in this one figure that no amount of people skills could allow someone to dive deeper than the surface. I suppose in his line of work, you have to create steel skin in order not to be hurt or taken advantage of. I had never thought of it that way before, but then again, since when does a customer think of the well-being of a worker? It's not often someone has the empathy for any line of work. That's where we lose ourselves even more. Customers are entitled. Customers are demanding and deserving of the services being offered, else they could go elsewhere. Yet the customers are not always right in situations, they simply want to be told they are. Customers don't like the truth. It's why the sweatshops thrive in other countries. It's why children work for pennies a day making horseshit products for folks with wealth. There's no fuckin' decency in us anymore. Our souls are outgrowing us, leaving us empty bodies.

I place a bowl of posole on the table, chili powder staining the air as the meat soaks in the broth. He stirs the soup for a moment before looking at me.

"I killed him. There's not much I remember, but I remember killing him."

The spoon languishes in his mouth for a moment. He hasn't eaten in a few days, maybe longer. I can see in his face that he enjoys what he has been given. He looks at me after another bite. "Why?" he asks.

There's no real answer I can give aside from what I am feeling at the moment. "I couldn't stand to see you like that. Drugged up. Abused. You deserved a better life than what he could offer."

There's a silence between us. It's stiff. Uneasy. I cough to break it, but there's nothing we can say to each other that is going to make this cold room warmer.

"You're in love with me. I've always feared it," he says flatly. "I could never let you in, D. But I guess with how we've met each night, the companionship, this all was inevitable. I wanted to disappear, D. I wanted a new life, away from sucking dick and getting fucked and whipped and beaten. I'm tired of the fantasies of men. I just want to live, and still I can't escape. You can't love me, D. You're a sweet guy, but you can't love me."

I felt like I was hit by a drunk driver in the south at four in the morning in July, flesh sweltering from the heat. He shattered my bones, slapped me on my good side, but he never wanted to return to me. I wasn't ready for his rejection, my hands shook, I want to get up, but I was wobbly. One, two, three, I begin to meditate to myself to calm my nerves, one, two, three. After a moment of repeating the numbers, my hands grow steady. I closed my eyes and took in a deep breath. I could feel my guilt trying to take over, but I must not allow it to. I am tired of him masturbating on my brain; I am tired of him stimulating all the wrongs inside of me. But nothing matters inside me right now.

"Then why do all the ticks inside me go silent when I'm with you?" is all I can ask, and there's a silence between us. He says nothing, he doesn't have an answer. I can't move on this time, but he is going to force me to. I can't. I just can't. He is still unobtainable.

"You have a bed here; you can stay, and heal yourself and be on your way when you're ready. I won't stop you," my composed nature continued. I get up from the table and retire to the office. My ghosts are outside now, they know I am alone. They've come to take me into the abyss and I will not be able to escape this time. They taste so good; I can't stop salivating at the thought of being devoured and ingesting the torture they have laid out for me. Nick, I suppose you won't be leaving anytime soon. And so it goes.

He slept on his own last night. I wanted to check in on him but I let him be. He left before I could wake up. No note, no signs of him being here, just gone. I suppose he grabbed some clothes to wear, or maybe he left some here, I don't know anymore. Some things are too trivial to keep note of. He is gone now—he has left me in a dead house. Maybe it'll be that way for a while.

There are some things we are simply not meant to have; he was someone I could never have in my life. But I wouldn't trade a moment of our time together. Little lab mouse, be safe on your travels, you won't always have a guardian to save you from the demons of this world. Though I am not much of a savior, not when I can barely save myself from the slow descent into the madness again. It's so hot in here.

I'm walking out of my door now, walking to the gas station to get my morning caffeine fix. Coffee is not strong enough anymore. I realized how weak it was for me yesterday, so it's time to make a change.

I meander my way through the store, the back lit up like the goddamn airport. I grab a can of energy and coffee; triple the amount of caffeine than I'm used to.

There's a cute guy behind the counter. I ain't seen him before. He's a border collie, young and tight like I always like them. But who doesn't? It's the fuckin' stereotype we look at when seeking others, it seems. He stood there watchin' me, brown eyes meshing with his brown fur. I walk up and set down the can, slam down some cash for the fix. I should probably buy these in bulk, but what the fuck do I know?

"You look like you need a beer instead of this shit," he comments as he's handing me the change. I stare at him for a second. I could smack the fuck out of him, but I don't 'cause he's cute. I smirk slightly and shake my head.

"When you've been dumped, you sometimes look like hell. It's life, kid."

He seemed young, but as the kids grow older, they start looking more mature than they are. I'm still lookin' him up and down though, undressin' him. I'm a dirty-minded man, it's what I do.

"Who could drop a cutie like you?" he responds with a wink. I'm not sure what it is or what the fuck just happened, but this jackass just hit on me for whatever reason. He puts his number on the receipt and says to call him anytime. I'm walking out of the station now, dazed. Downing the can of energy I jog home and place the number on my desk.

Maybe he's just lookin' for a hookup. Hookups are fun; I could go for another prayer session again. Nila, it's been awhile since I've seen you, I should return soon. All your followers return.

I grab the number and my phone and shoot him a text. So fuckin' impersonal. *You wanna meet?*

My phone vibrates with a response. The kid's quick. I don't know if he's eager or is fuckin' bored at work *I'm not an easy fuck. You'll need to take me out first,* he responds slyly. Probably some fuck lookin' for a free meal. I've paid way more for less, I suppose.

I could grab a bite. Tonight sound good?

It didn't take long for him to agree and give me his address. I don't know what it is with people. We live on moments, on shit that ain't even there, yet we fuckin' believe it will purify us. We answer only to our schools and our Bibles and our politicians, we put so much trust in others that we get burned way too often. Yet he trusts the world enough to go out tonight with me, and I'm not even stable for any person or thing in this universe. But here we are, makin' bad decisions through a fuckin' phone. Maybe he'll pull me from the abyss like Ely did. Maybe he can lift me from my ghosts. Maybe I'm searching for salvation in another black hole, but that's fuckin' life. We don't have much more than that. We just have fragments of time, how tasteless it feels to us. I stare at the morning through my window smokin' a cig, watch the neighbor-folk go on their morning walks and think of returning to work, but I still got a few days left of vacation. No need to go in early. The earth is still unsettled, give it time, dog, give it time to heal. I down the last of the energy, crush the can and dream of the fuck I'm going to have later. There's nothing else in this life to do, not for this low-life. Not today. Not in this life. But maybe, just maybe, I'm not as pathetic in the next.

www.ingramcontent.com/pod-product-compliance
Lightning Source LLC
Chambersburg PA
CBHW030537180626
46810CB00005B/1913